NUMBER TWO ★ GHOST TOWN MYSTERY SERIES ★ NIGHTHAWK, WASHINGTON

GHOSTOWNERS

Ghost of Nighthawk

BY CALAMITY JAN

Calamity Jan

For information contact:

WildWest Publishing
P O Box 11658
Olympia, WA 98508

Printed in the United States of America
by Gorham Printing, Rochester, Washington
Cover and book design by Kathy Campbell
Cover and text photographs by Jan Pierson

First WildWest Edition 2002

ISBN: 0-9721800-1-X
LCCN: 2002110774

http://www.calamityjan.com

Dedicated to my son, Blake,
who found the skull in the shack at Nighthawk—
and to his inquisitive son, Shane,
who shows every possibility
of following in his father's footsteps.

———

With special thanks to Juanita Cooksey
who took me through the town of her childhood
and told me its stories and legends, then
waited patiently for Nighthawk to come back to life.

———

And thank you, Teigen,
for inspiring me with those cool Mickey Mouse glasses.
I will keep them forever.

Contents

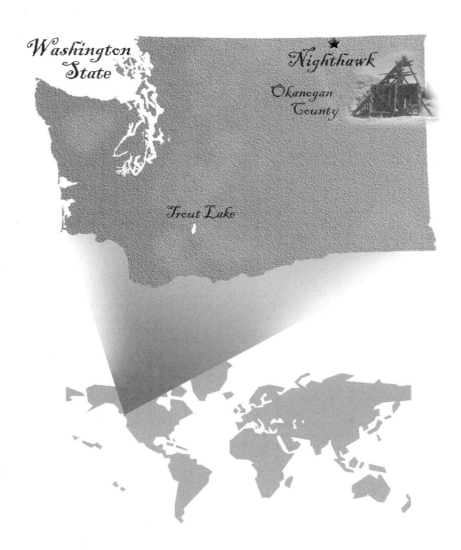

Washington State

Nighthawk

Okanogan County

Trout Lake

CHAPTER 1

The Shadow Stalks

Meggie and Paige walked up the graveled road, staring at the old shacks hovering like broken-down skeletons in the dusk. "*Night-hawk…*" Meggie said carefully, gazing around at the small ghost town in the north central part of Washington State. A few buildings were still standing—still hanging on like lost, dying creatures. Then suddenly, something caught her eye. Meggie froze. A shadow moved from behind a curtain in the upstairs window of a creepy old building just to her left. *Oh no…*

"Whoa!" Paige whispered, grabbing Meggie's shirt. "Did you see *that?*" Paige Morefield's eyes were as big as the moon that was creeping up from behind the gully. She tossed back her short bob of dark brown hair and turned to her best friend.

Meggie tried to answer—tried to tell Paige that she had seen it too. But she couldn't. The words were stuck like rocks in her throat. Her tall, slender frame stood rigid under the darkening sky, her dark blonde hair shivering in the shadows.

"Probably just the wind, huh?" Paige went on, like it was nothing.

"There isn't any—wind," Meggie said slowly, carefully.

Paige stared hard into Meggie's wide blue eyes.

Suddenly Meggie's aunt broke the silence, calling from the grove of locust trees where they had set up camp. "Meggie? Paige? Let's settle down for the night and do our poking around Nighthawk in the morning, okay?"

"Uh...sure!" Meggie replied, reeling around and racing back toward the van where her aunt stood unloading their sleeping bags from the small, wooden trailer carrying their gear. Paige followed in her dust.

"Aunt Abby?" Meggie skidded up to the van, glancing behind her shoulder. "Do you think there are any ghosts in Nighthawk?" There. She'd said it. But they had to know. They *had* to. *Maybe Nighthawk is different.*

"Ghosts?" Her aunt turned and faced her, a wide smile stretching beneath a frame of graying blonde hair. "That wild imagination in high gear already, Meggie Bryson?" she asked, pinning back a few stray wisps.

Twelve-year-old Meggie adjusted her glasses. "Well, after all, Aunt Abby, Nighthawk *is* a ghost town."

"That just means people don't live here anymore, Meggie. How many times have I told you that in all the years I've been researching and visiting ghost towns, I've never seen or heard a ghost yet. Now, you girls rustle up some dinner and I'll go down to the river and get some water."

Meggie knew her aunt was probably right. After all, she *was* an archaeologist and since archaeologists study ancient people and towns, she of all people ought to know. And what could be more ancient than a ghost? Meggie reached for the canteen and drew a deep breath, trying to push the stupid ghost thoughts out of her head. But it was hard. There had been *something* up there in that window. Something behind the curtain and Paige had seen it too.

Meggie shivered, even though it was still hot from the sticky August sun. *Could Aunt Abby be wrong just this once?* she wondered, watching her aunt gather up some containers and walk past the creepy old shacks down toward the river. Meggie lit the gas flame of the camp stove with an unsteady hand.

"I didn't see any nighthawks flying around out there at all, did you Meggie?" Paige asked, dropping the dry chicken noodle soup mix into the pan of water.

"Huh?" Meggie's thoughts shifted.

"Nighthawks. You know, those little birds they named this town after. Didn't the settlers call them 'bull bats' or something like that?"

Meggie turned to her best friend in complete amazement. Paige had already forgotten about the ghost and was now talking about those weird little birds like they were parakeets or something. If bull bats were anything like vampire bats, then there was a strong possibility they could actually suck a person's blood until they were almost dead. Meggie couldn't believe that Paige could actually be talking about these little creatures of death without so much as blinking an eye. Besides that, she could see that Paige had also forgotten about the shadow they'd just seen in that old building up the street. Meggie glanced over her shoulder and felt a chill.

"I wonder why they call 'em bull bats?" Paige went on, stirring the soup. "They're only birds."

Meggie grabbed a banana and sat down on a stump, amazed. "Only birds? In case you forgot, they named this town after those birds. The ghost town book says there's some weird legend about the nighthawks and that old guy named Haggerty who hid his gold." She glanced over her shoulder again, wondering why her aunt wasn't back yet.

"Which is why we're here, right?" Paige said, a slow grin teasing her lips.

Meggie shrugged and peeled the banana, getting her thoughts back on track. Paige was right. They had come to Nighthawk to see if they could find Haggerty's gold while Aunt Abby went off on another one of her archaeological digs. Meggie fingered her dark blonde hair thoughtfully, her mind backing up to the legend of the little hawk-like birds that hung around this river valley just below the Canadian border. And what about the legend? Was it true that James Haggerty had actually stashed some gold before he was run out of Nighthawk? Well, tomorrow they'd find out, wouldn't they? Meggie felt her skin prickle with the anticipation of what lay ahead.

But she was tired too. It had been a long, hot drive from their home in Trout Lake. Trout Lake and Nighthawk were at opposite ends of the state. In spite of the heat, it had been fun driving through the North Cascade Mountains, then up the Okanogan River that wound like a snake and led them to this little ghost town nearly hidden in the hills. Mines, scattered around like skull eyes, seemed to watch them. When the van pulled into Nighthawk, she *knew* they'd made the right decision to come.

Gray, skeleton bones of crumbling dwellings lined up along the graveled street to greet them. Yes. Meggie *knew* this was going to be one fantastic vacation. She tried to shut the stupid ghost thoughts from her mind and focus instead on the gold and all the fun they were going to have searching for it. After all, her aunt said there weren't any ghosts in ghost towns, anyway. The shadow might have been a cat sitting on the windowsill. Or maybe a bat hitting the curtain. *Get a grip, Meggie.*

Her aunt returned with the water, and after they finished eating and setting up camp, they said their goodnights and crawled into their tent. Aunt Abby sat by the kerosene lantern outside, finishing some research papers before she turned in. Meggie switched on their battery operated lantern and began to read a ghost town book, but all she could think about was that shadow she and Paige had just seen up in that window. This place might be fun, but would it be *safe?* she wondered. Even in the bright light of morning when the hot sun beat down, would it be safe for them to explore Nighthawk? Or did the ghosts and bull bats or—whatever-it-was they'd seen up in that window—only come out at night?

Are the nighthawks flying now? she wondered, laying down the book, finally. *Are they flying over that creepy old place where we saw the shadow? And what about the shadow? What if it wasn't a bat or a cat or a nighthawk? Is there a chance somebody or some THING might be watching us? Aunt Abby is an archaeologist, not a Ghostowner like her and Paige. How could she know for sure?* Meggie realized her aunt knew a lot about artifacts and archaeology, but did she know anything about ghosts?

Finally, her aunt turned off the lantern. Moon shadows crept down through the locust trees, hovering like ghostly hands over the tent. Meggie heard the van door slam shut and knew Aunt Abby would be in her sleeping bag and asleep in minutes. Just like Paige.

Meggie pulled the sheet over her face, hoping she could shut out the thoughts flying around in her head like bull bats.

CHAPTER 2

The Accident

Eerie shadows slid in and out of Meggie's dreams. She felt thankful when morning crept down into the river valley and chased the shadows away. *Ghosts be gone, it's time to find your gold, Mr. Haggerty,* she said with a grin, slipping on her cutoffs and shirt and stepping out into the bright morning sun. *It is time.*

"Thanks for breakfast, Aunt Abby," Paige said after they finished their cereal.

"I think I can handle a box of dry cereal and milk," Aunt Abby laughed, trying to control her frizzy hair that was always falling into her face. "But that's about the only cooking I'm good for." She plopped her wide-brimmed straw hat on her head and began gathering up her supplies. "Let me see—camera, laptop computer, trowel, G.P.S. unit, calculator, magnifying glass, first aid kit, maps, scale..." She stuffed her nylon pack full of gear.

Meggie grinned and finished her glass of milk. Paige always called her "Aunt Abby" too, even though she was Meggie's aunt. But that was okay. The three of them sort of fit together. They loved exploring ghost towns and although this was only the second ghost town for the two of them, Meggie felt like she and Paige were full-fledged Ghostowners already.

Her aunt was so cool. Even though she was pretty old, she was a lot more fun than most kids. She wore funny straw hats, high top sneakers, baggy shirts and trousers and didn't seem to mind when Meggie and Paige let their food and apple cores get moldy under their sleeping bags and stuff like that. That was probably because she loved to dig in the dirt and hang out in ghost towns just like they did. But her aunt was smart, too. She had tons of college degrees. Aunt Abby told them that being a consulting archaeologist meant she usually had a lot of freedom and since she specialized in ghost towns, that her job was also fun. Aunt Abby searched for artifacts and made important discoveries for the different people or agencies that hired her. Even though Meggie knew she was lucky to have the best parents and family anybody could ever have, there probably wasn't a person on earth as fantastic as her aunt.

Except maybe Paige. Paige Morefield was definitely the best friend a person could *ever* have, and Meggie knew she was lucky. Even though Paige was a few months younger and shorter than Meggie, she was extremely brave. Paige could watch scary movies on TV and *never* blink an eye. If you were going to be hanging out in ghost towns, Paige was the person to have along. The only way Meggie knew Paige was scared was when her eyes got big. And that didn't happen too often.

It did last night when they saw the shadow, though, Meggie remembered. And it would happen again if they saw that—that *whoever*-it-was up in the window of that old building. Or it might happen if they got trapped in one of the Nighthawk mines looking for that gold. Especially if a bull bat or that ghost got to them before they got to the gold—or whatever it was that old miner had hidden before he got run out of town. Meggie felt her pulse start up again and was glad when breakfast was over and they could be on their way.

"Watch out for rattlesnakes," Aunt Abby said, hitching up her bulging nylon backpack. "And don't fall into some old well and drown." She unhitched the trailer from the van, then locked it. "You have everything you need?"

They nodded.

"And you have the key, Meggie?"

Meggie nodded again, patting the rear pocket of her cutoffs. Aunt Abby was the best. Her aunt probably worried sometimes, but she never let on. It was best, too, because exploring ghost towns could be pretty dangerous. Most adults would have heart attacks if they knew about all the stuff that had happened to her and Paige.

Aunt Abby climbed into the van and waved. "You kids have fun now. And do what you have to do, because we have to leave tomorrow."

"Tomorrow?" Meggie's shoulders fell. That was hardly enough time to find the gold.

"I'm going into Chesaw to pick up some groceries and do some errands. I won't be long," she called out. "The old man who owns a lot of this property around Nighthawk gave me permission to stay and do some digging, so check with him if you need anything while I'm gone." She pointed to an old house on the edge of town. "Julian Cooksey. Yes, that's his name."

Meggie nodded and caught up with Paige. Her best friend sauntered past the run-down buildings on the one-and-only street running through the town. "Julian Cooksey. Chesaw. Nighthawk. What weird names, huh, Paige?"

Paige didn't seem to be paying too much attention. She kept tossing her hair out of her eyes, gazing around in the eerie, quiet heat. "Let's take the short cut behind these old shacks," she suggested, pointing toward the barren grass and rocks and trees that dipped down toward the river.

Meggie agreed. She didn't want to be walking past that scary old building again anyway, even if it *was* broad daylight. She felt a shiver just thinking about that shadow they'd seen the night before. A lady in the store up the road at Loomis told them that Nighthawk was one of the loneliest places on earth, and from the looks of things, she was beginning to believe it was true. Meggie took off running, her sneakers catching the rhythm of her heart. Pounding. Racing.

Paige was close at her heels, leaping over bunchgrass and rocks and broken-down fences. They hurried behind the decaying pink house and Livery Stable toward the bridge that crossed the Similkameen River.

"I'm almost positive that was the Nighthawk Hotel where we saw that shadow last night," Meggie said breathlessly. "Last night when I was reading the ghost town book, it said there was a hotel on the main street and it's the only building big enough for that. Do you think it *might've* been a ghost, Paige?"

"Aunt Abby said there aren't any."

"But how does she know for sure? She's never even been to Nighthawk."

"She knows a lot, Meggie. It was probably just one of those little bull bats. You know, a nighthawk."

Meggie shook her head, straight blonde hair rustling like dry grass in the morning wind. "If you want my opinion, I think it was waaay too big to be a nighthawk, Paige. Somebody or *something* was up at that window looking down at us. Anyway, I think nighthawks only come out at night and it wasn't quite dark yet. Night. Nighthawks. Don't you get it?"

Paige shrugged and Meggie wondered if her best friend just wasn't getting it. She watched Paige slow down and kick a loose, prickly mound of sagebrush like she was in a soccer game at school.

"Paige," she said, slowing down. "This could be serious."

"Yeah?"

"Yeah," Meggie replied.

Paige shrugged and started across the bridge. "It could also be fun if we don't freak out every time we see a shadow."

Meggie drew back and frowned. But, maybe Paige had a point. She caught up with her best friend, glancing over her shoulder one last time. The creepy old hotel was only a shadow now.

"Most of the gold mines are supposed to be on this side of the river, aren't they?" Paige asked, walking along the road beside Meggie. She pointed upward where the sage and tree-dotted hills stretched toward the sky.

Meggie nodded. She could see that Paige had already forgotten about the shadow in the window, which was probably a good idea. *We're Ghostowners.* she reminded herself. *Authentic searchers for secrets, gold, old mines and other treasures.* Yesss.

"Didn't Aunt Abby tell us those mines had names?" Paige asked.

Meggie turned to her friend.

"I think she said that the one closest to Nighthawk is called the

18

Caaba—or something like that."

"Okay. Yes—and there's another one called the Ruby and the third one is—is..." Meggie bit her lip, trying to remember the third mine.

"The Six Seagull Mine. Yeah, that's it," Paige told her.

Meggie stopped in her tracks and turned to her friend. "The Six EAGLE, Paige."

"Eagle, Seagull, what's the difference?" Paige said with a shrug, tossing her hair out of her eyes. "Except that the Eagle-Seagull Mine had the most gold, didn't it? Maybe that's the mine we better be looking for."

"Paige..."

"And how come that old miner named Haggerty got run out of town?" Paige went on.

Meggie's mind backed up, trying to remember what she'd read in her ghost town book. She walked on, thinking. "I think there was another mine—a fourth mine. Yeah, that's it. Haggerty and some of his buddies in Loomis and Nighthawk were trying to sell it."

"So?"

"It was a bad mine. There wasn't any gold—except the people who wanted to buy it didn't know that. They were going to pay a lot of money for a mine that wasn't worth anything."

"Whoa, " Paige brightened. "Now things are beginning to get a little more interesting. What happened, Meggie?"

"I guess one of Mr. Haggerty's problems was that he liked hanging out in the saloons too much, and Nighthawk and Loomis had a *lot* of them in those days. Anyway, one night he had too much whiskey and gave the secret away and because of that, these dishonest guys at Loomis and Nighthawk lost the sale. They lost a lot of money and were real mad."

"Then what happened?" Paige inched closer.

"I guess this guy who raised sugar cane near Loomis brought a jug of his sugar cane molasses to the saloon to show it off, but dumped it all over Haggerty instead. Another guy ran upstairs and got a feather pillow and slit it open and then they rolled him in those feathers and ran him out of town. The story says he never showed up again, except when they buried him near Nighthawk."

"Yesss!" Paige gestured, giving her the high five. "Now we're getting somewhere. So, did Haggerty already have the gold hidden? Or did he sneak back later and hide it?"

"I don't know," Meggie told her. "The legend wasn't very clear about the gold."

Paige sighed. "We only have one more day, Meggie," she muttered. "*One day.* It's not enough time."

Meggie knew she was right. This ghost town vacation was too short. If they were going to solve the mystery, then they had to do it fast. They hiked up the road, gazing at the broken down dwellings that were now just memories of a lost, forgotten era. Meggie noticed an old house with a bunch of junker cars in the yard to her left. "Looks like somebody still lives there." She gave her friend a nudge. "I guess this town isn't completely deserted after all, huh Paige?"

But Paige hadn't heard. She had crossed the road and crawled under a barbed wire fence, motioning Meggie toward an abandoned house. Meggie's heart skipped. *Better not be haunted.*

"Whoa! And will you look at *this?*" Paige called out. "A wellll..."

Meggie froze. One minute Paige had been standing ten feet in front of her and the next, she dropped out of sight.

CHAPTER 3

Brave Rescue

"Helllp!" the faint voice called out from below. "Get me outta here!"

"Paige!" Meggie cried, racing over to the hole that had swallowed up her best friend. She adjusted her glasses and peered down. Her heart fell. She saw only blackness. "Oh, Paige—are you okay?"

"I won't be if you don't get me out!" Paige yelled up, her words nearly consumed by the dust and black earth engulfing her.

Meggie could hardly think straight. She stared into the hole that dropped into darkness. "Is—is there water down there?"

"No, thank heavens! But it's gross! Hurry, Meggie! Do something!"

"Yeah! Okay!" Meggie cried, trying to stay calm. A cold sweat crawled down her back. *Now what?* Suddenly a thought slithered into her head and hit her like the sting of a viper. *Snakes. This is central Washington State. Rattlesnake country. Timber Rattlers. Oh no. No.*

"Get a rope Meggie! Anything!" Paige called again, her voice faint. "Hurry!"

"*HURRY!*"

Meggie whirled around, her wide blue eyes darting frantically in every direction. Except for some sagebrush and a few scrubby pine trees scattered around, there was nothing. *Nothing.* "Don't move, Paige!" she cried out. "I'll get something! I'll be back!"

Her feet took off running back toward the house with the junker cars, thankful this town wasn't completely deserted. *They'll have a rope,* she knew, swallowing the wind in short, breathless gasps. Meggie leaped onto the porch, pounding on the door until her knuckles hurt. But no one was home. "Oh nooo!" She whirled around, searching frantically for some rope. Anything! "Please...something...please!" But there was nothing. Nothing but a bunch of junk and empty cars gazing up like rusty hollow-eyed skulls.

Meggie wiped a nervous sweat from her face and took off running back toward the bridge—back to the campsite. The trailer. There would be rope and stuff in there. Yes! Sweat poured down her face and body as she raced toward the town—cutting behind the old buildings once again. Nearing the campsite, she fumbled in the pocket of her cutoffs for the key. But it wasn't there. She threw her hand against her head and skidded to a halt. "Oh no! Nooo! I left it in my jeans!" Her jeans and clothes were locked up tight in the little wooden trailer smack in front of her face. "Now what?"

Meggie's mind reeled. "Wait a minute! That man. Yeah...that old guy who gave us permission to be here! Yes! Yes! Aunt Abby said to check with him if we needed anything. Sure. He'll help. He'll have a rope!"

Hope flooded Meggie's senses. She turned and started running for his house in the distance, wind stinging her face. Dust and rocks flew as she raced down the road and up the rutted driveway toward the ramshackle house.

"Anybody here?" she cried, nearly falling through the old porch. "Hey! Helloooo?" She pounded on the old door. "Anybody home?" But there was no answer. No sound except the hot wind hitting her cold sweat and sending chills clear down to the soles of her feet.

She steadied herself against the doorframe, breathing hard. "Find a rope, Megan Bryson!" she screamed silently, racing back down the driveway. "Find something and get Paige out before it's too late!" Loose gravel flew and stung like bees as she made tracks back to the main street of the deserted town. *Now what?* she wondered, gazing around in the eerie silence. "Wait a minute. What about one of these old shacks? Okay, maybe I can find something in one of these old dumps! Sure, why not?" Meggie's thoughts raced, her hopes rose. It wasn't like she was breaking and entering, since there weren't many windows or doors left anyhow. Besides, there were no signs telling them to keep out.

Then Meggie remembered the cabin. Whoa. Yes! Directly across from the hotel. Maybe people stay there during the summer. "They'll have a rope. Sure! Oh please! Please!" she cried, racing across the grassy knoll that separated the fork in the road. But, no one answered her frantic knocking.

"This *is* a ghost town!" she cried. Suddenly she noticed an old shack with a door hanging by its hinges—hanging half-open like the tongue of a dying creature. Meggie swallowed her fear and raced toward the dwelling. Breathless, she ducked in, cobwebs curling around her neck like phantom fingers. Her eyes squinted in the clouded shadows as she searched frantically for a rope. Wire. Anything. But there was nothing except old cans and garbage and dusty, rotting boards strung around like bones. A skull in one corner stared at her as though she had invaded his house. She paled and backed out of the freaky old dump. *Was it human?* she wondered grimly.

"I can't believe this!" she cried as she ran into the next shack. And the next. But the old stores or saloons or livery stables were nothing but ghosts of the past. Empty. Vacant.

Meggie paused to catch her breath, leaning against some rusty old farm machinery parked under a shed. Then she looked up and stared across the street. The hotel. The creepy old hotel where she and Paige had seen the shadow the night before. A lump caught in her throat.

"Okay...okay..." she said carefully "Maybe there's a rope in there. Or something to make a rope like—like..." Meggie tried not to choke on the words forming in her head, she tried not to choke on the truth she knew she must face. *Like old curtains...*

Zombie-like, her eyes moved upwards to the old curtains in the upstairs window. Her flesh crawled as the image returned—the shadow, moving slowly—then disappearing behind the curtains the night before. *Those curtains—knotted together—a rope.*

Meggie gripped the spoke of a huge antique tractor and braced herself. She knew what she had to do.

"For you, Paige. For you."

She gritted her teeth, then ran across the street to the Nighthawk Hotel. Hot air circled her throat, river bugs stung her face. But it didn't matter. Paige mattered now. She had to make a rope. Get her out of the well. And okay, if there was someone behind that old rag of a curtain up there, then he—*it*—would just have to move aside.

Meggie couldn't believe she was doing this. She wasn't the type. It was Paige who knew how to scare off German Shepherds and Pit Bulls. Paige would have gone for the curtains in that old hotel first. She would have told the person—or—or IT to get out of the way and she would've ripped those curtains off the rods like it was *nothing*.

"Oh, Paige!" Meggie cried, climbing over the metal gate and heading toward a dusty window that hung half-open. "I'm coming! I'm coming!" She gripped the splintery frame and squirmed into the narrow opening.

Trembling, she wiped the dust from her face and gazed around the huge room littered with old furniture and junk. If she could just find what she needed in this room, she wouldn't even have to go up those freaky stairs. *Okay, rope...rags...anything.* Meggie raced through the junk-strewn rooms on the first floor, but she found nothing. "Oh, Please! Please! I don't want to go up there. I can't!" A cold sweat crawled like a snake down her spine. *A snake. Right now Paige might be wrestling a rattlesnake. Or fighting off black widow spiders.*

Fear seized her senses. *Get a grip, Meggie.* She knew what she had to do. She would go up those stairs and get those curtains. If there was somebody up there waiting, then that was just too bad. The worst thing that could happen was that she might die of a heart attack. Paige mattered now.

She grabbed the rickety old banister and started up the stairs. Up...up...up....

Nighthawk Hotel

CHAPTER 4

The Creepy Clue

Meggie's blood raced faster than the Similkameen River running behind the town, but she did it. She actually climbed up the crumbling stairs and entered one of the rooms without at least fainting. Rotting wallpaper curled down like fingers in the small, musty room furnished with only a rusty iron bed and nightstand. Gripping the darkened brass doorknob, she steadied herself and stared at the old window framed in ragged curtains of a bygone day. She leaped on to the bedsprings and started pulling them down, running from room to room, window to window. Meggie knew she must get enough fabric in order for the curtain-rope to reach her friend. Paige had fallen a long way down.

At last Meggie reached the last room at the end of the hall. She stopped for a moment, feeling the cold trails of sweat crawl down her back. Was this the room where they had seen the shadow the night before? She drew a deep breath. It didn't matter. Paige mattered now. Meggie rushed across the room and grabbed the ragged scrap of curtain hanging over the window above one more broken-down bed. The rod came flying down with the shredded cloth, hitting her on the head. Her glasses went flying.

"Owww!" she yelled, glaring at the stupid thing that had just clobbered her. Arms loaded, she kicked it aside, then started out of the room. "Hey, wait a minute. My glasses!"

Meggie whirled around, searching for her glasses. Suddenly, something caught her eye. She stared down at a piece of paper that must have fallen out of the curtain rod. Quickly, Meggie dropped the curtains and picked up the scrap lying on the floor. She tried to read it but her hands were shaking too hard. "Okay—okay. Later." Shoving the crinkled piece of paper into the pocket of her cutoffs, she picked up the armload of curtains and raced down the stairs and out the door.

"Yahooo!" Meggie yelled, running through the town and over the bridge. "I did it! I did it!"

But her excitement faltered when she reached the silent hole. She drew back, afraid to call down—afraid that if she did, there might not be an answer. "Pa—Paige?" she called out finally. "Are you okay?"

"Where've you *been*?" Paige called out from the dark pit. "I thought you'd never get here!"

Meggie's heart fell with relief. She's alive! "Oh, Paige! I'm so glad you're okay!" Hands trembling, she began to separate and braid the curtains.

"Well I won't be if you don't hurry up and get me out of this slime pit! There are THINGS crawling all over down here. Yuck, it's *gross!*"

Her grouching sounded wonderful. "I'm making a rope from those curtains we saw up in those windows! I'm hurrying as fast as I can!"

Silence.

"Paige? Are you okay?" Meggie yelled down, tying the final knot on the curtain rope.

"You mean you went up in that freaky hotel? Up where those curtains—where that shadow…?"

"Yeah," Meggie told her, sprawling on the ground and throwing the makeshift rope down to her friend. "It was nothing."

Another silence followed, then Meggie felt the sudden jerk.

"Got it!" Paige yelled.

Relief flooded Meggie's senses. Her knuckles whitened as she braced herself against a rock and began pulling her best friend up...up...up—until at last she reached the top.

Covered with dirt, Paige crawled out, blinking in the bright sun. "Arrugh!" she snorted, leaping around and frantically brushing things off her dirty shorts and shirt and skin and hair. "I'm goin' swimmin'!"

Meggie collapsed on the ground, exhausted. She was so happy, she could have hugged Paige right there on the spot. But she didn't. She figured she'd let her wash off the black widow spiders and gunk in the river first. Meggie got up and followed Paige down toward the rivers edge. Clothes and all, she jumped in behind her dirty, happy friend. A small, protected pool encircled them both as they splashed around like a couple of crazy coyotes.

"Ooops!" Meggie cried, backing out of the water and reaching into the pocket of her cutoffs. She'd almost forgotten the piece of paper that had fallen out of the curtain rod up in that hotel room. She threw her wet hair out of her eyes, hoping it wasn't too late—hoping the water hadn't washed off the words.

"What is it?" Paige asked, pushing her short strings of dark hair out of her eyes and coming toward her.

"A note or something. It fell out of the curtain rod up in that hotel. Almost killed me."

"The note almost killed you?" Paige climbed up onto the bank beside her.

"No, the *curtain rod*, Paige."

"Oh. Well, what's it say?" Paige climbed up onto the bank beside her, pushing her wet hair out of her wide, inquiring eyes.

Meggie's hands shook as she pulled it close and began to read the faded, scratchy old words that looked as though they could have been written over a hundred years before. She spoke carefully, slowly.

"WOOD YOU FOLLOW ME TO THE NIGHTHAWKS
OVER AND UP AND UNDER AND DOWN
BUT WAIT FOR THE MOON
AND SOON"

"Whoa!" Paige almost fell over. "Do you think...?"

"Hey, yeah," Meggie nodded, her hands still shaking with excitement. "The clue. I'll bet anything it's the clue to Haggerty's gold!"

CHAPTER 5

The Listener

"I heard that," the voice said.

Meggie reeled around and stared at a lanky kid standing on the bank behind them. A huge tin dish hung in one hand. He'd been panning for gold. And listening.

"I heard everything. It's the clue, isn't it?" The slow, cocky smile started moving up one side of his sun-tanned face. "I'll find it now. I'll find the gold." Brown hair shivered like dry, burnt grass in the wind.

Meggie's mind raced, wondering if it had been him hiding behind those curtains in the hotel the night before. Was this smart-mouthed jerk the one who'd been watching them all the time?

"Who are you?" It was Paige now. She had walked up to the guy who was a good two heads taller, facing him like she was Batman and he was Chicken Little.

"I'm Jay Paul Leeberg, who're you?" he snorted, throwing a towel over his shoulder

"I'm Paige, and this is my friend, Meggie. How come you were eavesdropping?"

"Excuse me? In case you didn't know, I was here first," he said, not blinking an eye. "Swimming and panning for gold. How come you busted in on *me*?"

Meggie's throat tightened. *He knows. He knows about the clue. He heard us, didn't he? He'll find it. He'll find the gold before we do. Unless...*

"Would you follow me to the Nighthawks...Over and up and under and down but wait for the moon. And soon..." the kid said, repeating the clue word-for-word. The arrogant grin was still stuck like a leech on his face. Slowly, he began backing up, his neon green swimming trunks catching the reflection of the river behind them.

Paige turned to Meggie, silent panic exploding in her wide brown eyes.

"No, don't go!" Meggie said. "Uh—um...if you stick with us we can—uh, we can find it together!" She threw wet strings of hair out of her wide eyes.

"Meggie!" Paige cried out, grabbing her arm. "How could you?"

Meggie couldn't believe she was talking like this, but what choice did they have? If they didn't hang out with this guy, then maybe he'd find the gold without them. It probably *was* him up in that hotel room the night before. He probably lives in Nighthawk—maybe in that old house with all the junker cars, or—or that cabin. And now that he has the clue, he'll know exactly what to do next. Where to go.

Clear, cold blue eyes matched Meggie's gaze. "Get real," he snorted. "Why should I hang out with you? I don't need to waste my time panning for a few nuggets anymore," he laughed. "Now that I've got the clue, I can find the gold myself, thank you very much."

Meggie's heart fell. She squinted against the sun, watching him turn and saunter off through the dry weeds and grass toward the road that crossed the bridge into town. The silver dish swung back and forth like it was a shield and he was the haughty, victorious knight who had just won the battle.

"The sleaze-ball has just ruined everything," Paige said the minute he was out of sight. "What a nerd!"

Meggie agreed one-hundred per-cent. "Which means, we have to find it before he does, that's all," she said, reaching for her glasses.

"But if he lives around here, then he probably knows exactly where to go. Didn't you hear him, Meggie? He said he'll find it now that he's got the clue."

"Whoa..."

"What is it?" Paige asked.

"My glasses! My glasses are back in that dumb hotel! They fell off when the curtain rod clobbered me."

Paige sighed with relief, brushing dark strings of damp hair from her face. "I thought it was something serious."

"It is serious."

"Weren't they your old ones? Don't you have your good pair back in the van?"

"Well, yeah."

"Good, because I'm not interested in going into that creepy 'ol dump and look for your glasses, are you? Who needs two pair anyway?"

"They were my Mickey Mouse glasses." She knew it sounded stupid for a twelve-year-old to talk like this. *Feel* like this.

"Yeah, and you've had 'em for a hundred years, too. They were cool when you were eight, Meggie. But now that you're twelve, they aren't cool anymore. Besides, they don't even fit. Those wire frames are ready

32

to snap and send Mickey Mouse flying anyway."

"I *know*, Paige. But they're perfect for ghost towns," she went on, still knowing it must sound stupid. How could she explain it? After all, they were her very first pair of glasses. She'd picked Mickey Mouse over Barbie, Batman and the Little Mermaid. She loved the way the little mouse blended right into the pink wire frames. Besides everybody needed an extra pair of glasses, and these were sort of *faithful*. Losing her Mickey Mouse glasses was sort of like losing a part of herself.

Thankfully, Paige changed the subject.

"It was *gross* down in that well, Meggie. There could've been rat snakes, rattlers, scorpions, coyotes and who knows what else down there." Paige started toward the bridge.

Paige's gruesome words brought Meggie back to reality. Losing her best friend was a lot more serious than losing her Mickey Mouse glasses.

"You don't think it was an old mine shaft, do you?" Paige went on, pulling her sticky, wet t-shirt away from her damp skin.

"Naw, probably a well."

"One thing for sure, though," Paige went on, "I am *definitely* watching my step from now on. Echh."

Then Meggie's thoughts shifted to the bigger problem at hand. Jay Paul Leeberg. "We have to get to that gold before that dorky kid does," she told Paige.

"Oh yeah, I almost forgot about *him*."

"I think he's intelligent," Meggie said, jumping over the fence. "He had that clue memorized in seconds."

"Yeah. Disgusting, huh?"

Meggie nodded. "If it'd been a real dense guy listening in, then we probably wouldn't have a problem. But Jay Paul Leeberg isn't dense. I can tell."

"Me too. Maybe he's already got it figured out." Paige slowed down, facing her best friend.

"Yeah, so that's why we have to find him," Meggie told her. "That's why we have to follow Jay Paul Leeberg wherever he goes."

CHAPTER 6

Mickey Mouse
is Missing

It didn't take long to locate Jay Paul. They saw him walking into the cabin across from the Nighthawk Hotel, a red Ford Bronco parked in front.

"Whoa, wait a minute," Meggie said, grabbing Paige's shirt. "That rig and those people weren't here this morning. Or when we came last night. Which means, it couldn't have been Jay Paul up in the hotel last night."

Paige stopped, then glanced up at the hotel across from the Leeberg cabin. "Too bad. I thought we got rid of the ghost."

"Yeah, so did I," Meggie said, gritting her teeth.

"Well if you want your glasses, Meggie Bryson, then you're gonna have to go up there and get 'em yourself. That or say goodbye to Mickey Mouse forever."

"Aunt Abby says there aren't ghosts in ghost towns."

Paige wasn't buying it.

"She should know, Paige."

"Okay, yeah—sure. But there *was* something looking out at us from behind that curtain last night, remember? And you're the one who said it couldn't be a nighthawk."

"I can't believe you're acting like such a wimp, Paige. It isn't like you."

Paige turned to Meggie.

"If you remember, it was *me* who went up there all by myself less than an hour ago. I got those curtains so that I could rescue you. Nothing grabbed me, Paige. The place was empty. It was *nothing*."

"Yeah?" Paige turned to her, clearly impressed.

"So, now it's your turn to go up in that hotel. You go on up and get my glasses and I'll wait over behind that machinery in those storage sheds across the street and see if Jay Paul goes anywhere. One of us has to be on the lookout." Meggie hurried across the grassy mound that separated the main street before Paige had a chance to answer. "The last room at the end of the hall!" she called back. "Upstairs."

But it was Meggie who was impressed when Paige returned. Covered with cobwebs and dirt, her best friend actually looked relaxed. It was like she had just explored a haunted house and was ready for lunch.

"They're not there," Paige said, trying to brush the gunk off her damp shirt and shorts. Then she looked up and pointed to some little bird alighting on the wire of an old telegraph pole nearby. "Hey, Meggie—look! Are those nighthawks? I thought nighthawks only came out at night."

But Meggie couldn't think about nighthawks right then. "Not there? What do you mean my glasses aren't there?"

Paige turned to Meggie and shook her head. "I looked everywhere.

36

What a creepy old dump."

"They have to be there. The room at the end of the hall. Upstairs."

"Yeah, and they weren't. Guess Mickey Mouse took off," she said, the trace of a smile on her lips.

"That's not funny, Paige."

"Hey, come on, Meggie. We're after the gold, not your Mickey Mouse glasses."

But somebody did take my glasses, she said through tight lips, *which proves there was somebody or some THING up there after all.*

"Did he come out of the cabin yet?" Paige went on.

"Huh?"

"Did Jay Paul go anywhere?"

But before Meggie could answer, she saw him coming out of the cabin with a man and an older kid. She grabbed Paige's arm and squeezed it tight. Ducking behind an old combine, she and Paige watched as the three got into the red four-wheel drive vehicle. "I'll bet that's his dad and his brother," Meggie whispered.

The Bronco pulled out onto the gravel road, passing the shed where they crouched, hiding. In minutes it disappeared, winding up the Loomis Highway south of town.

"Whoa, we're in luck!" Paige laughed, grabbing Meggie's arm. "He's outta here. It's time to make our move!"

"All right!" Meggie agreed, giving her the high five. "Aunt Abby's back. Let's go grab some lunch and map out the plan."

"Who says we need Mr. Cool Jay Paul to help us find the gold!" Paige laughed, following Meggie down the road toward camp.

Suddenly, an old man appeared almost out of nowhere. Meggie noticed he walked with a limp and used a stick for a cane. "That might be the old guy Aunt Abby told us about," she whispered to Paige. "The one who gave us permission to hang out around Nighthawk."

"Julian Cookie?" Paige asked.

"Cooksey."

They stopped as the old man walked toward them. It was a good thing the wind wasn't blowing because if it had been, Meggie figured the poor old guy would've blown away then and there. His arms and legs looked like crooked spaghetti that was about to break. "Hello," she said, hoping he wasn't the talkative type. Time was wasting. They had to figure out that clue and find that gold.

"Eh?" He leaned toward them, struggling to hear. Struggling to see.

"Hello!" It was Paige now, and Meggie knew she knew how to talk real loud for hard-of-hearing people since her grandma was that way. Except Paige's grandma wasn't *at all* like Julian Cooksey. Paige's grandma would probably use a cane for a baton in her aerobics class.

"Thanks for letting us hang out around Nighthawk," Meggie said, trying to keep her voice loud enough so he could hear.

"Hang?" He gazed around, shading his eyes from the sun and looking worried.

"Oh no," Meggie said, "I didn't mean *that* kind of hang. Uh..."

"Thanks for letting us come to Nighthawk!" Paige said, sounding like she was yelling through a loudspeaker at a ball game.

"Oh yes. A fine place, eh?" he replied, his eyes and face crinkling into a large smile. "I used to run that there hotel." Julian Cooksey pointed to the old hotel with one hand, wiping a stray tear with the other. "By dang, I miss 'em, though," he muttered.

"Miss who, Mr. Cooksey?" Paige asked.

"Millie and the girl. Millie, she was my wife."

Meggie drew a deep breath, staring at the old man with tattered clothing and shoes. Safety pins held the front of his old blue shirt and his gray hair hung in strings. He needed Millie. He needed *more* than Millie.

"Say, you two want me to show you around Nighthawk, eh?"

"Oh no!" Meggie said quickly. "Uh—we have some stuff we have to do. But thanks for asking." He was so sweet. Maybe later when they had some time.

"I could take you in that there hotel and tell ye about every visitor clear up to '47 when it closed down. Old Ed McNull built it back in the boom days for the drummers—peddlers we call 'em now," he chuckled.

Peddlers? Meggie glanced at Paige. *What the heck are peddlers?*

"Things were rosy then, yes indeed," the old man went on. "The Vancouver, Victoria and Eastern were runnin' their line smack dab through Nighthawk. Yup. An' when the Nighthawk Mill got crankin' full blast, the Ewings took over the hotel. Turned it into a boarding house for the mill workers, they did. After they were all gone, Millie and I started up the hotel again." His raspy words picked up speed. "Had to kick out the Voetberg and Schissler tribes that first week, though. They jest about tore up Room 8 and 9 upstairs." He chuckled and stood up a bit straighter now.

"Danged if I don't still hear that fancy Miss Prentice Abigail makin' that 'ol piano sing like a banjo. My little Cassie..." "He faltered, reaching for his hankie. "Little Cassie could play too, oh yes she could."

Meggie couldn't believe this. She felt so cruel interrupting his story like this, but they *had* to go. "Mr.—Mr. Cooksey? Uh, I know..."

"Eh? You do?" He brightened and drew closer, wiping his eyes once more. "You know about my little Cassie? You heard from her, have you?"

"Who's Cassie?" Paige asked, her eyes searching the old man's weathered face.

"Paige, we have to go," Meggie said between tight lips.

"Eh?" He cupped his had behind his ear and leaned forward.

"Mr. Cooksey, we have to GO," Meggie put in. This was terrible, but they had to leave Nighthawk the next day. Jay Paul might return any second now. There just wasn't much time left.

"Go? Oh—they did up and go all right, but cain't say as I blame 'em. Dang fool I was back in them days. Too many fancy ladies and saloons in Nighthawk and Loomis. 'Cept was my own fault. Millie jest up and left, she did. Took my sweet Cassie too." Tears started spilling down the wrinkled old face and the dirty hankie just made things worse. "Seven years old and sweet as could be. Never saw her again."

"Oh, Mr. Cooksey..." Paige said, reaching for his old arm that held the cane steady. "You mean you never saw your little girl after that?"

Meggie's throat tightened. *The poor old man.* But they had to leave, didn't they? They would come back tomorrow, though. Yes. Before they left Nighthawk, he could tell them all about Cassie and Nighthawk. But, tomorrow—*after* they found the gold.

The old man turned to Meggie who began to back away. He nodded and his frail smile told her it was okay. That he understood. "Well, enjoy Nighthawk now," he said, turning slowly and walking away.

"We will, Mr. Cooksey. And thanks," Meggie called out. Her voice cracked. "Right now we have to go somewhere, but when we get back you can show us around, okay? And tell us about Cassie."

But he hadn't heard. She watched him hobble back down the street with his cane and could have sworn his shoulders had dropped six inches.

"Oh, Meggie," Paige said, grabbing her arm. "That poor old man. What happened to Cassie? Maybe we should have listened."

Meggie hurried toward the campsite. She felt terrible. Worse than terrible. She had just brushed off this kind old man like he was a pesky mosquito. If they weren't in such a hurry, she'd never, ever do a thing like that. They didn't have a choice. They had to find the gold before that dorky Jay Paul did. This was their last chance. She had to put that old man out of her mind for now. *She had to.*

Meggie and Paige almost collided with Aunt Abby who had just finished lunch and was leaving again.

"You're filthy, Paige. Did you fall in a well?" she asked, frowning.

"Yeah, but I didn't drown because there wasn't any water in it," Paige told her. "I did get gunky, though, but this dirt isn't from the well because I jumped in the river and washed that dirt off. I got this dirt from the old hotel down the street."

Aunt Abby appeared confused.

"She was looking for my glasses," Meggie said, still trying to get her mind off that poor old man. "My Mickey Mouse glasses."

"You lost them?"

Meggie nodded.

"Well, you look like you've just lost your best friend. Weren't those your old ones?"

Meggie nodded again. "Oh, Yeah. They were my Mickey Mouse glasses. They fell off when I got bonked on the head up in that old hotel getting curtains to make some rope to pull Paige out. That's when the clue fell out of the curtain rod."

"Then you didn't find them?"

"You mean the clue?"

"No, your glasses."

Meggie shook her head. "No. They're gone."

Aunt Abby plopped her straw hat down on her frizz of hair. "Oh well, at least you've got your good pair, but whatever you do, Meggie, don't lose *them*. Your parents will kill me if they have to buy you new ones for school." She opened the glove compartment and gave her the good pair.

"Thanks," she said, wondering how they kept getting off the subject.

"I'll be at a site south of town near the river," Aunt Abby said, pausing. She had a twinkle in her eye.

Meggie recognized the pause. The twinkle. It happened whenever her aunt wanted to get historical. Meggie hoped Aunt Abby was in a hurry so the historical part wouldn't take too long.

"Did you girls know that before the white fur traders came to this area, there was an Indian trail along the Similkameen River?"

No, Meggie shook her head as she slipped on her glasses, glancing at Paige who had a blank expression on her face. She didn't know. Neither did Paige. And right then they didn't really care about the Indian trail. Maybe after they found the gold...

"It was one of the routes connecting Fort Okanogan on the Columbia River with the Canadian towns on the Fraser," Aunt Abby went on. "It was used by the Indian tribes of the inner valleys for trading expeditions with the costal Indians. This valley may be rich with artifacts. I've got my papers and permission for the dig and I should be back by dark. Now you two stay out of wells, mine shafts, and old hotels, hear?" she smiled and climbed into the van. "And tell me about your clue tonight, okay?"

"Okay," Meggie replied, thankful her aunt hadn't gotten carried away this time. She and Paige had to hurry. Suddenly she remembered the key. "Ooops, did you leave the trailer open, Aunt Abby?"

"Yes, but don't you have the key?"

"Left it in my jeans," she replied sheepishly. "In the trailer."

Her aunt rolled her eyes and drove off. "Lock it when you leave," she called back.

"Bye, Aunt Abby," Paige said, pulling out the cooler. She began making the peanut butter sandwiches while Meggie read the clue one more time.

"WOOD YOU FOLLOW ME TO THE NIGHTHAWKS

OVER AND UP AND UNDER AND DOWN

BUT WAIT FOR THE MOON

AND SOON"

Meggie repeated the words carefully, smoothing out the crinkled note on the portable table. "This guy couldn't even spell," Meggie told her, staring at "WOOD" and knowing he should have spelled WOULD. "Okay now, it says—Follow me to the nighthawks...over and up and under and down. Whoa. Hey!"

"What is it?" Paige almost knocked over the jar.

"Over and up Do you think that means over the bridge and up? Up the mountain?"

"Mmm. Sure makes sense to me," Paige replied, handing Meggie a sandwich and wrapping two extra ones for their trip.

"I'll bet that's it. Besides, there's nowhere to go but up. This whole

43

valley is surrounded by mountains."

Paige reached into the cooler and got out six cans of soda, stuffing four in her pack and handing one to Meggie. "But up to where?" she asked, opening up her can and taking a big swallow.

"And under what and down where?" Meggie added, realizing this could be a lot more complicated that she first thought. "FOLLOW ME TO THE NIGHTHAWKS. OVER AND UP AND UNDER AND DOWN... Okay Paige, let's go! We have to find this gold before dark!"

Paige took a bite of her sandwich. "Whoa, Meggie!"

"What's the matter, Paige?"

"BUT WAIT FOR TH—THE MOON..." Paige struggled, peanut butter sticking to her words.

Suddenly Meggie's eye grew wide—wider than the moon that would be hanging over the valley tonight. "The *moon?*"

"Yeah, Meggie. We have to wait for the moon."

"And then?" Meggie's heart started pounding so loud, she could hardly hear her own words.

"And then—then maybe the *nighthawks* will tell us."

CHAPTER 7

Lofty Shadow

"Hey, wait a minute!" Paige said, swishing her peanut butter teeth clean with her pop. "What's a nighthawk look like? I mean, how are we gonna get our message from a nighthawk if we don't even know? These little birds we see flying all over the place *might* be nighthawks, but then again, they might not."

Paige was right, Meggie realized. She got up and started rummaging through the trailer, looking for Aunt Abby's box of books.

"And how come the early miners called 'em bull bats, Meggie? Maybe that's something important we need to know."

"You think maybe it's because they're sorta big, like bulls are bigger than cows?" Meggie asked, trying to keep the giant vampire bat thoughts out of her head.

"Who knows?" Paige cleared off the paper plates and cups and threw them into the garbage. "Too bad the person who wrote up that clue didn't choose another kind of bird like a robin or chickadee or something."

Paige had a point. But they couldn't sit around and complain about something that might have been done a hundred years before. They had to move fast—before Jay Paul Leeberg got back and beat them to it.

Finally Meggie found the book on birds and looked up **Nighthawk.**

"Okay—it says: *A slim gray or gray-brown bird with long pointed wings, slightly forked tail and white wing patches. They become active just before dark and when they dive,* their *wing feathers produce an odd musical hum. Although they prefer flying at night, they also fly during midday. The male has a white bar across its notched tail and a white throat. Sits on wires, fence posts and rails. Sometimes called bull bats."*

"Yesss ," Paige said. "So these cute little things we see zooming all over this place *are* nighthawks after all!"

"Yup," Meggie replied, closing the book in relief. "Thank heavens bull bats are *nothing* like vampire bats. Not even close."

"Huh?"

"Nothing."

"This isn't gonna be scary *at all*," Paige said, grabbing some granola bars and fruit and stuffing it into her backpack with the extra sandwiches. "Those cute little birds are going to give us the secret, too." A slow grin spread across her tanned cheeks. "Tonight."

Meggie grabbed a pencil and some paper and wrote a note to her aunt and stuck it under a rock on the table. "Just in case we don't get back before dark," she said to Paige.

"Yeah, just in case," Paige agreed, adding a flashlight and insect spray into her overstuffed backpack.

Meggie caught he best friend's gaze, knowing there was a strong possibility they weren't going to be back before dark since they had to wait for the moon. But Aunt Abby would understand. She always did. She, of all people, understood how ghost towns just got into a person's bloodstream. After Meggie finished writing the note, she pulled a few more supplies out of the trailer, including a fold-up shovel, a rope and a small pick. *We'll find that gold—oh yes we will,* she said to herself, securing the shovel and rope in her backpack and handing the pick to Paige. *We have to. We have to find it before Jay Paul does.*

"What's the rope for?" Paige asked.

"That's just in case you fall into another hole." Meggie grinned, pulling her long blonde hair back into a ponytail and knotting it. She hitched up her pack, then locked the trailer and slipped the key into her pocket.

Paige rolled her eyes and sighed.

"Let's move."

They cut behind the old buildings, stepping around rock scabs and weeds and scraggly pine trees. "Thank heavens Jay Paul isn't back yet." Meggie knew they had to hurry.

Paige paused and turned back once more.

"Come on," Meggie prodded.

Her friend just stood there.

"Paige? What're you looking at?"

"Mr. Cooksey's place."

Meggie caught her breath. *Mr. Cooksey?* She'd been trying to get Julian Cooksey out of her thoughts and he just kept hobbling back in. Paige wasn't helping.

"I just can't stop thinking about him, Meggie."

"I know," she replied with a slow nod. "I can't either."

Paige drew a deep breath, then turned back toward the mountain, cutting between the livery stable and the old house with peeling pink paint. "Poor old man."

"We'll make it up to him," Meggie told her.

Paige hesitated.

"But later. We have to get the gold first, Paige. First things first, okay?"

"The gold. Yeah...sure." Paige nodded and started out once more.

They hiked across the bridge together, gazing upward at the sagebrush and pine-covered hills. "OVER AND UP," Paige said carefully, pulling Meggie away from thoughts of Julian Cooksey. "OVER the bridge is the easy part, but UP could be a problem. UP could be anywhere up there."

Meggie agreed, gazing up the miles of hills that had been slashed down the center with the blue-green knife of the Similkameen River. She wrapped her arms around her slender frame and shivered as they walked up the road. Paige was right. That's why they had to use their heads and figure out this clue. She glanced back at Jay Paul's cabin behind the livery stable in the distance. Suddenly, she saw a shadow out of the corner of her eye. Meggie froze.

"What now?"

"I—I..." Meggie couldn't finish.

Paige whirled around, dark hair flying. "What'd you see back there, Meggie?"

"A shadow. The livery stable. Someone up there—in the loft..." Her words were getting caught like sagebrush in a barbed-wire fence.

Paige turned and stared at the old building at the foot of the bridge. "You're kidding."

"Come on!" Meggie said, whirling around and taking off like a bull bat. "Someone's watching us! Someone's up in that loft watching us!"

They raced up the dusty road, then under a fence and toward the abandoned house near where Paige had fallen into the well.

"We'll hide in here!" Meggie cried, crawling over a splintered windowsill and through a huge, broken pane of glass. Her sweat turned cold in the shadows as she stood panting. Breathless.

"Are you *sure* you saw something?"

"I'm positive, Paige!" Meggie's words came fast. "N-Now we know the truth! Now we *know* somebody's been spying on us from the first night we got here!"

Paige's eyes grew wide. "Maybe it's just him! Maybe Jay Paul never left and it's him following us. Or maybe they just got back!"

"No Paige. We would've seen their rig driving into Nighthawk. No. It's not Jay Paul. It's someone else. Or some *thing* else." A chill crawled down her back.

Paige swallowed hard. "You think somebody might know we're after the gold?"

Meggie nodded. "Why else would they—IT—be following us?"

"But it couldn't be a ghost," Paige said firmly, yet her eyes were still as round as an owl's. "Ghosts don't care about gold."

"How do you know?"

Paige couldn't answer and Meggie knew that was because they didn't know a thing about ghosts. She wanted to believe Aunt Abby. She wanted to believe there wasn't any such thing. But Nighthawk was different. Meggie had sensed something eerie the first night they had walked down the street and seen that shadow in the window of the old hotel. Maybe she wouldn't be feeling so weird if her Mickey Mouse glasses hadn't just disappeared into thin air. And now this.

"So what next?" Paige climbed over some old planks and furniture and peered out through some rotting slats of wood.

Meggie wished she knew. *Do we just race back past that old livery stable and try to hide in the tent or some old dump until Aunt Abby comes back? Do we leave Nighthawk forever, never knowing? Never finding the gold?*

"We have to keep going," Paige cut into her bleak thoughts. "Up the mountain. He won't see us once we get over that ledge behind those rocks and trees." She shoved some cobwebs aside to get a better look, gazing upward onto the green and brown hills. "If we find the gold, Meggie, do you realize you could buy ten thousand pair of Mickey Mouse glasses *and* that horse you've always wanted?"

"I don't want any more Mickey Mouse glasses," Meggie said. "I just want the ones it took."

"Maybe a nighthawk flew in the window and took 'em. Nighthawks probably eat mice."

"Paige, that's stupid. A nighthawk isn't going to pick a Mickey Mouse off each side of my pink wire-framed glasses and eat them. Anyway, what're we doing talking about my Mickey Mouse glasses when death could be on our heels?" Meggie brushed a creepy web from her face. "Gross!"

Paige shrugged. "Okay, then let's just find the gold, Meggie. Whoever's snooping on us won't find us once we get over that ridge. Those trees up there are going to hide us."

"Unless..." Meggie couldn't finish. No, it can't be the ghost. Aunt Abby would've known. She has tons of college degrees which means she'd definitely know whether ghosts exist or not. She's been digging up artifacts in ghost towns for years and said she's never run into one yet. Never. "Okay," she said to Paige, "let's go for it. I'll count to three."

Paige nodded as they moved toward the open door frame on the back side of the house. Her eyes were still as round as an owl's at midnight.

"One...two...three!"

Meggie and Paige took off running, dust flying in every direction. They skirted the sagebrush and scrub pine, moving up the rise toward the ridge.

"Hurry!" Meggie called out to her best friend. "Hurry, Paige!"

Abandoned House

CHAPTER 8

The Foom

In minutes they had reached the ledge and jumped into a wide gully hidden by trees. "They can't see us now." Meggie braced herself against a rock, sweat covering her face. "We're safe! At least for now."

Paige threw her dark hair out of her eyes and gazed around. "Let's have a soda," she said.

"Paige."

"What's the matter? Aren't you thirsty?"

"Well, yeah, but..."

"Good. Me too." Paige pulled two cans out of her backpack and handed one to Meggie. "They're still cold."

Has she already forgotten about the shadow in the loft? Meggie wondered, taking the can and opening it slowly. She watched her friend walk around and drink her soda like they were having a picnic in the park.

"What's that?" Paige asked, pointing to a long wooden trough winding up the side of the mountain.

Meggie shifted her thoughts and glanced up at the sun-parched remains of the old wooden conveyer that limped upward like an old wooden snake. "Hey, wait a minute. I think that's a flume."

"A *what?*"

"A flume," Meggie repeated. "They used to carry water."

Paige frowned, shading her eyes from the sun. "Where to?"

Meggie wasn't sure. Why would somebody need water up here? Were flumes supposed to send water up? Or down? *Oh well, it doesn't matter.*

"Should we follow it Meggie? It's going up the mountain." Paige pointed toward the rotting fragments of the trough moving in a winding, upward path.

Meggie stared at the thing, then pulled the clue out of her pocket again. *Is there some connection to this flume thing?* she wondered, unfolding the yellowed paper. They had to follow this clue closely. They couldn't just follow flumes and go mountain climbing for weeks on end.

Paige broke into her thoughts. "Once we're out of this little gully and start climbing again, that guy or—or whoever it is down there is gonna see us,"

Meggie realized she might be right. "If that happens I think we're far enough ahead that we'll have time to get away and hide."

"Maybe." Paige shrugged.

Meggie walked over to the ledge and peered over. There was no one in sight.

"So do we just follow that Foom thing up the mountain?" Paige asked.

"I'm not sure," Meggie replied, unfolding the clue and reading the words once more. She realized they had to do something. There wasn't much time left. "After UP comes UNDER," she said, "and then DOWN, right? If that's the case, then after we get to the top, we go under. But under what, Paige? Then down. Down to where? If DOWN means down the mountain, does it mean down the other side? Then where would we be? I mean, there might be a hundred valleys." Meggie was getting more confused by the second.

"Tonight the nighthawk will tell us," Paige said carefully.

"Just like that."

"That's what the clue says."

"So, how will the nighthawk tell us?" Meggie knew her voice sounded thin, but sometimes Paige acted like everything was so easy.

Paige shrugged. "But whoever wrote that clue should've used a parrot instead of a nighthawk. Then we'd know. Yeah, wouldn't that be cool, Meggie? *To the left, girls, then ten paces...*"

"Paige."

Paige shrugged.

"Whoa! Wait a minute!" Meggie cried, staring at the clue once more. She almost choked when she saw it. The note trembled in her hands.

"What's wrong?"

"Look! WOOD you follow me...WOOD, Paige! Not WOULD but WOOD!"

"So?" Paige took the paper from her hand and examined it more closely. "So the guy couldn't spell."

"Maybe he could!" Meggie tried to hold back her excitement. "Maybe we follow the *WOOD*, Paige!"

Paige threw her hand over her mouth, then whirled around and stared at the old wooden conveyer leading up the mountain. "The wood? You mean that wooden thing? Yes, I'll bet that's it! We follow that Foom, right?"

"Flume," Meggie corrected, her voice trembling like her tall, lanky frame. "We—We follow the wood. WOOD YOU FOLLOW ME... Wow! Hey, wow, Paige!"

"Yessss!" Paige burst out. "We got it, Meggie Bryson! *We got it!*"

Meggie's hands shook as she placed the clue back in her pocket. Stuffing her empty pop can into her backpack, she caught up with Paige who had already started climbing. Skirting rocks and scraggly pine and juniper, they followed the flume, scrambling like gophers upward in the dust and heat.

Now and then Meggie gazed back over her shoulder to make sure they weren't being followed. But Nighthawk slowly faded into the valley and before long, she couldn't even see the buildings anymore.

Not even Mr. Cooksey's old place at the edge of town.

Meggie drew a deep breath. She didn't want to think about Julian Cooksey. She didn't want to think about the way she'd acted, the way she'd brushed him off. She tried to forget the expression on that kind old face when she'd told him they didn't have time to listen to anymore of his stories. Meggie turned away from the valley below, hoping thoughts of Julian Cooksey would fade just like the buildings and river and trees below. But they didn't. It was as though the old man was climbing this mountain with them. Stumbling. Still trying to talk. Still trying to tell them about that little girl...

"Can you see if that red Bronco is back?" Paige asked, cutting into Meggie's troubled thoughts. Paige had paused and was gazing down from a rock.

Meggie's thoughts shifted. "Huh?"

"The Bronco. Can you see if it's back?"

"No," she said, wiping some sweat off her face and squinting against the sun. But it didn't matter. Jay Paul and whoever-it-was in the livery stable weren't any problem now. From this far away, she and Paige might just as well be a couple of coyotes or mule deer. Only the Similkameen River, winding between the cottonwood and willow trees below, was visible now.

By late afternoon they had nearly reached the crest. "I can't believe we've climbed this high," Paige said, plopping onto the ground. She pulled out some sandwiches and handed one to Meggie, fanning herself with one hand. Her hair stuck to her moist face in dark brown strings. "And we're gonna make it before dark, Meggie. We are." Brown eyes flashed. "Time enough to check things out while we WAIT FOR THE MOON..."

"AND SOON..." Meggie added, grinning. She wiped some sweat off her neck with her white tank top and took a huge swallow of her soda. They were directly west of Nighthawk. *So far, so good.*

"Who'd ever think a Foom was leading us to the gold?" Paige shook her head and stared at the old wooden conveyer that continued moving up the mountain.

"Flume," Meggie said.

"I think the Indians would've called it a Foom."

Meggie turned to Paige and frowned. "These things were probably built a long time after the Indians were here, Paige. The Indians probably never even knew or cared about Fooms."

"Flumes," Paige corrected.

Meggie turned to Paige and they locked eyes, then suddenly broke out laughing.

"Foom, Foom, Foom and away!" Paige hollered, getting up and zipping her pop can around like it was an F-15 fighter jet.

"Wait a minute, Paige," Meggie went on, grabbing her shirt. "*Think.* Why build a flume if you're not moving something up or down? There has to be a reason to send water or whatever it was down, right?"

Paige's small chin dropped.

"Like a settlement. A mining camp."

"Whoa, that's right," Paige said, stuffing her empty pop can into her pack. "Miners and Mines go together. *Gold* mines."

"Exactly," Meggie said carefully, her pulse quickening. "What do you bet this is that gold mine Haggerty and some of his buddies tried to get rid of?" Meggie couldn't finish her sandwich fast enough.

"Wait a minute," Paige grabbed her shirt. "Wasn't that a bad mine, though? I mean, if this is the mine he wanted to get rid of, then there won't be any gold up here, will there?"

Meggie hadn't thought of that. She shrugged and hitched up her pack. "Let's find out, Paige. If this clue means anything, then it's not going to matter how things look. Maybe Haggerty decided to play one last trick and let the joke be on them. Maybe that mine still had a rich vein."

"Yeah, maybe that's what happened. I wouldn't want anybody to roll me in molasses and feathers," Paige said. "Aunt Jemima's maple syrup might be okay, though."

"Paige..."

Paige shrugged and walked on.

Slowly, carefully, they began the final ascent. What would be waiting at the end of the flume?

CHAPTER NINE

The Tomb

And just before they reached the ridge, they got their answer. The ruins of an old mining camp lie nestled in a small, well-hidden ravine. Meggie shivered with excitement, staring at the rock tailings piled up like ghost mountains. Rotting timber framed the entrance to the mineshaft and hovered like pale, dead bones. Beyond, the remains of a few miners' shacks lie scattered around.

"Will you look at this?" Meggie said, moving slowly toward the forgotten gold mine and abandoned corpse-like dwellings. "A secret mine, Paige Morefield. Tucked up here neat as can be. Are you thinking what I'm thinking?"

"Yup," she replied, pointing to an old sign hanging by one nail.

Meggie turned to the hand-carved wooden sign dangling on a rusty old peg, creaking back and forth in the wind. She strained her eyes against the shadows of the sun that had now dropped behind the mountain. "NIGHTHAWK MINE," she repeated the words slowly, then threw her arms into the air. "Yesss! This is it!"

"WOOD you follow me to the NIGHTHAWK..." Paige's words were

like music—like the wind singing through the pines—like the hum of the little birds diving.

And the nighthawks were everywhere, Meggie realized, gazing around. *Everywhere.*

"Yesss! We found it, Meggie!" Paige threw her pack into the air. "We found the last part of the clue!"

Meggie felt dizzy with excitement. She could hardly believe it. Now she knew how the miners must have felt when they struck gold.

"UNDER...we go under next, Meggie. I guess that might mean Under the WOOD frame?"

Paige's words cut into Meggie's thoughts like the sharp beak of a bull bat. She watched Paige walk toward the hand-hewn timbers framing the mineshaft, the crumbling, forbidding entrance to the black mine. Her body grew rigid.

"And then DOWN," Paige went on. "I'll bet that means down into this mineshaft."

Meggie drew back. .

"And we'd better do it real soon," her best friend went on. "Before it gets too dark. It's gonna be a long hike back down tonight. We don't want Aunt Abby to worry."

Meggie's throat tightened as she stared into the black tunnel behind the crumbling timbers.

Paige motioned for her to follow. "Let's go, Meggie. This is probably it!"

Meggie had noticed the sky beginning to fade into an eerie gray dusk. Her unsteady hand pulled out her flashlight as she caught up to Paige. It wasn't exactly that she felt scared, it was just that she wasn't used to mines. Especially not pitch black ones.

Meggie and Paige locked arms and moved slowly into the black mouth of the mine, stepping carefully over rotting planks and dirt. "Watch for snakes," Paige said. "I'll bet anything they're down here. Snakes hang out in gullies and holes and places like this. Rats too."

"Paige, would you mind talking about something else?" Meggie asked, knocking some freaky webs aside with her flashlight.

"Yuck. I hope those are just cobwebs and not black widow or brown recluse spider webs."

"*Paige!*" Meggie stopped and glared down at her best friend.

"You asked me to talk about something else."

"Something *nice*, Paige."

"Like all the stuff we can get when we find the gold?"

"Yeah."

"Okay. I'm getting a CD player, a phone and TV set for my room," Paige said. "I'd also like to get some real cool clothes and..."

"On second thought, maybe we better not talk so much down here, okay?" Meggie suggested. "We shouldn't use up the oxygen." She wasn't sure if that would be a problem, but it sounded like a pretty good possibility. At the moment, a CD player, phone, and TV set didn't seem like they should be on the Ten Most Wanted list. The wrong step—the wrong turn could mean Zip. This creepy tunnel was worse than a haunted house.

The dry, musty air grew thinner as they moved through the hollow, empty chamber. Meggie stepped carefully over debris and rotten timbers that had collapsed, lying around like gruesome fingers waiting to grab them. Her flesh crawled. In minutes they reached a sudden drop. The hole fell into the darkness. Meggie squeezed Paige's arm, pointing the flashlight downward.

"*Gross!*" Paige groaned, drawing back. "Snakeville. Well, so much for the CD player and my own phone. I mean, if this is the DOWN part of the clue, then *forget* it."

Suddenly Meggie spotted a long wooden plank over to her right. It was lying like a narrow bridge across the chasm, stretching to the tunnel beyond. "Look! A little bridge," she said with tight words, trying to slow down the thumping of her heart. Meggie crawled toward the plank suspended across the black hole. "May—Maybe DOWN is further on, Paige. Come on."

"Wait a minute. Wait a *minute!*" Paige blurted, drawing back. "Not me. I've had enough black holes for one day."

"It's no different from the balance beam at school," Meggie said, amazed at her bold words—her sudden rush of courage. She released Paige's grip and knelt down, taking the lead in a slow crawl across the plank. "It's actually wider than the balance beam," she went on, trying to keep her words from quivering like her knees.

"Then if it's like a balance beam, how come we're crawling?" Paige asked, keeping close behind.

But before Meggie could answer, a huge crack split the timber and sent both girls plummeting into the darkness below.

Nighthawk Mine

CHAPTER 10

The Pit

"Hellllp!" Paige yelled, landing smack on top of Meggie.

Meggie choked, trying to catch her breath, hoping she'd wake up from the worst nightmare in her entire life. She felt the weight of Paige slide off her back, listening to the echo of her scream, the thundering of her heart.

"Meggie?" Paige groped around in the shadows, grabbing her shirt. "Are you okay?"

Snakes. Meggie leapt up, feeling her feet begin to dance. *Oh gross! They're probably crawling all over down here.*

"Meggie!" Paige called again, her voice edged with panic now. "Are you okay?"

"Yeah," Meggie called back, breathless, terrified. "Are you?"

"Uh huh," Paige replied, grabbing the flashlight that had fallen out of Meggie's hand and rolled to one side of the pit. Meggie watched as Paige beamed the light around in a circle, checking for creatures.

"This is *horrible!*" Meggie sputtered, knowing her best friend's eyes were probably huge by now. Now Meggie realized what it must have been like for Paige when she had fallen into the well that morning. She jerked off her backpack, frantically groping for the insect repellent.

"Two holes in one day is too much," Paige said, beaming the light upwards to see how far they had fallen. "But at least we're together, Meggie. We've got each other."

Meggie wasn't sure if that was making her feel any better. But at least she'd found the spray.

Paige started choking. "Meggie! Quit that! Quit bombing me with that gunky spray! I can't even see!"

"It'll protect us!" Meggie sputtered, turning the spray on her own face and arms and legs. "Do you think it'll get the snakes?"

"If I go blind from insect spray then I'll never know if there are any snakes down here. And I won't be able to see how far we fell." Paige beamed the light up over their heads.

Meggie paused and gazed up, then caught her breath. "My glasses!" she burst out, realizing they'd fallen off. Paige beamed the light around until Meggie found them. Grabbing her last and only pair, she put them on her slightly turned-up nose and gazed upward once again. "How'd we fall that far and not get killed? Paige—this is terrible! Even with my glasses I can hardly see the top! W-we could be trapped in this black hole. *Forever!*"

The flashlight trembled in Paige's hand.

"The rope!" Meggie said suddenly. "We'll make a loop in the rope and throw it up. There should be something up there we can hook it on to."

Meggie reached into her backpack, grabbing the rope. She formed a loop and knotted it. Hands trembling, she threw it upward into the darkness. But each time the rope fell back onto the earth-rock floor with a quiet, sickening thud.

"Here, let me try!" Paige said, handing her the flashlight and taking her turn.

Meggie beamed the quivering light upwards and watched. The rope wasn't even getting *near* the top. She knew it was hopeless. *We're trapped. Trapped in a lost mine. Nobody knows we're here. We might die right here in this black hole...*

Finally Paige dropped the rope. Meggie heard her breathless sigh. Felt her fear. "Paige?" she said, as soon as she could get the words to come out straight. "Maybe we can climb out. Maybe we can find rocks we can use like steps." She groped her way toward the wall, shining the light around.

"No," Paige said in a hollow tone. "Look, Meggie. See how this hole gets smaller as it goes up. Like an upside-down ice cream cone. And there are no rocks down here. There's no way."

Meggie shone the light around, knowing she was right. Tears began to creep out from the corners of her eyes as she walked over to her friend. "We can't give up, Paige. We *can't.*"

Paige didn't answer. Meggie reached out to her best friend, the tears coming freely now. She felt Paige's silent tears, the fear that was flooding both of them now.

"I don't even *care* about a stupid phone in my room!" Paige burst out. "Or the coolest clothes in school. I don't care about anything except seeing Mom and—and even my dad."

Meggie drew back, listening. Paige never talked much about her dad. She said she never cared about him after he'd walked out on her and her mother and married somebody else. Except when they were in California exploring Bodie. Paige talked about him for the first time then.

"The *stupid* gold!" Paige went on, her voice exploding with anger and fear. "If it wasn't for that dumb clue, we wouldn't even be here! Maybe there are more dumb people like us who think gold is such a big deal. Maybe they're all just a bunch of bones lying around—like we're gonna be!"

"No, Paige!" Meggie cried, refusing to think about turning into skeletons this soon. Twelve was too young. It just wouldn't be right. "Don't talk like that! We *can't* give up, we just can't!" But Paige was right about the gold. Who cared anymore? *Let the stupid little night-hawks keep their gold or whatever it was they were hiding.*

Time crawled like a slow, cold coffin being dragged to its final resting place. Sometimes Meggie threw the rope up, hoping and praying for a miracle. But the only answer in the dark, gray tomb was the sickening thud of the rope falling back on to the dank earth floor.

She glanced at her watch and knew it was probably getting dark outside by now. Would Aunt Abby be starting to worry? Meggie flicked off the flashlight so the batteries wouldn't run down. Fear and despair hung like a shroud. What difference did it make if the batteries went dead?

She listened to Paige yell for help for the hundredth time, wondering if her friend's throat was as raw as hers. They both knew it was dumb to be yelling. Maybe the nighthawks heard, though. Maybe they'd be the only ones who would ever know what happened. She kept trying to force the bleak thoughts out of her head, but it wasn't easy.

Including thoughts about old Mr. Cooksey. Meggie wouldn't ever get to listen to any of his stories about Nighthawk or find out what happened to Cassie. She wouldn't ever get a chance to apologize and tell him that *he* was a lot more important than the gold. Her eyes brimmed. *I'm sorry, Mr. Cooksey.*

Suddenly Meggie's thoughts skidded to a halt. She heard a sound. Overhead. Faint, but it *was* something. Someone. She grabbed Paige's frozen arm, knowing Paige had heard it too. What was it? A bat? Some animal that had picked up their scent? She cringed at the gruesome thought. Or was it something even more dangerous? Had this clue deliberately led them into a trap?

She couldn't breathe. She couldn't move.

CHAPTER 11

The Nighthawk Speaks

"Hey! Somebody in here?" the voice echoed in the hollow tunnel overhead.

"Oh my gosh!" Paige and Meggie cried out, jumping up and beginning to yell their heads off. Deafening echoes exploded everywhere.

Meggie couldn't believe this. A miracle.

"Down here!" she hollered, her pulse pounding like the footsteps that were coming closer. Closer. "Be careful! Don't fall in like we did!"

Paige grabbed the flashlight and shone it overhead. Quivering like cave bats, light shadows slid up the walls, then disappeared in the black-mouthed hole overhead.

Suddenly the footsteps stopped. Meggie's throat tightened as she watched Paige's light move toward the form peering down.

"Hey," the voice said. "You two sure do choose one heck of a place to hang out."

It was Jay Paul. Jay Paul Leeberg! Meggie couldn't believe it. It *was* a miracle!

Paige threw up her arms and started leaping around like a frog while Meggie just yelled "I could hug you!" over and over and over again.

"If you hug me, I'll leave," the voice said as soon as the hollering died down.

The cavern fell silent.

"Oh no! That's not what I meant!" Meggie cried out. "I just meant I'm so *happy*. If you hadn't showed up, we could've turned into bones," she went on. She knew her words probably sounded sickening, but right now she'd hug King Kong if he'd be willing to pull them out.

"Do you have a rope?" Paige called up.

"No."

"We do," Meggie said. "But we can't get it up that high. It's too far."

"I'll be back!" he called, the sound of his footsteps fading into the silent tunnel overhead.

Meggie and Paige turned and grabbed each other, then started jumping and laughing until they were almost crying.

"You crack me up, Megan Bryson!" Paige laughed, wiping dusty tears off her face.

"Huh?" Meggie paused.

"Hug Jay Paul Leeberg?" She giggled.

"You know what I meant!" Meggie snorted, her ponytail swinging back and forth in the shadows.

"Yeah," Paige said, grinning. "But it's still pretty hilarious."

The girls finally stopped laughing and jumping around. "I wonder what he's looking for?" Paige asked. "You don't think he's going all the way back to Nighthawk, do you?"

Meggie scarcely heard her words. "He followed us, Paige. Can you believe Jay Paul actually followed us up this mountain?"

"Hey, that's right," she replied. "But I'm glad he did! I mean, if he wasn't so sneaky, we'd be bull bat dinner."

Meggie hated to admit it, but Paige was right. But how did he do it? How did he keep out of sight like that? Maybe he knew the land a lot better since he'd been coming up to the cabin with his folks. He probably knew exactly which rock and bush to hide behind. *Maybe that was him back in that livery stable, too.*

They waited in grateful silence. What more could they say?

"Hey," he called down, returning at last. "Did you guys find the gold yet?"

"No, and we don't care if we ever do!" Meggie burst out.

"Right!" Paige added.

"But have you checked it out down there?" he went on. "The clue says DOWN. Maybe you're down in the hole where it's hidden."

Meggie reddened. How could he be talking about the gold at a time like this? "Maybe this is the hole where we could've died," she said with icy words.

"Yeah. Okay. Just thought I'd check."

Meggie snorted, her nostrils flaring with disdain.

Jay Paul went on. "Okay, now here's the plan. I got this big ol' branch which I'm gonna lower down into this hole as far as I can. Your job is to try to hook your rope over one of the snags. Just start throwing, okay?"

"Not a bad idea." Paige turned to Meggie.

Meggie shrugged, tossing the rope upward. It missed.

"Just keep trying," he said. "And keep the light out of my face. I need to see what I'm doing."

Paige and Meggie took turns tossing the rope until it finally hooked on a limb.

"There!" he yelled, pulling it up slowly, carefully.

Meggie bit her lip, watching the rope uncoil like a snake at their feet. Relief flooded her senses.

"Got it!" he called down.

"What now?" Paige cried, echoes bounding everywhere.

"After I make a bunch of knots for you to climb up on, I'll secure the rope around a rock up here. Then you climb up one at a time."

"You go first," Meggie said. She wasn't sure if she was being brave or chicken. But it didn't matter. The important thing was, *they were going to make it.* They weren't going to turn into twelve-year-old skeletons after all.

"You sure you want me to go first?" Paige asked.

Meggie nodded and held the rope steady, watching her best friend climb up the makeshift ladder, one knot at a time. Her pulse throbbed with hope. *Be careful, Paige. Careful...*

"Yahooo!" Paige hollered the minute she reached the top.

Relieved, Meggie secured her backpack, flicked out her flashlight, then grabbed the rope.

"Okay. Okay, I'm ready!" she yelled, her voice as taut as the rope. Slowly Meggie began the climb. Her heart pounded with every step, every knot as her lanky frame moved upward, knot by knot. Up. Up. Up.

"Thanks! Hey, thanks a lot!" she said to Jay Paul the second she was up and over the ledge. "I mean, I'm so, so glad you followed us." This didn't sound too cool, but she really did feel thankful. Meggie wanted Jay Paul to know she wasn't just saying words that didn't mean anything. She watched him nod and step back, coiling up the rope in his hand. *He probably thinks I'm gonna hug him,* she realized, feeling like a dweeb. "Okay—yeah, so let's split!" she sputtered, pushing the humiliating thoughts aside with a huge shrug.

In minutes they were out of the mine and standing under the night sky. Meggie gazed up at nighthawks dive-bombing everywhere. "Look!" she said to Paige and Jay Paul. "Those little birds are zooming around like they own this place. No wonder they call it the Nighthawk Mine." She gazed around, watching them alight on a huge tree at the crest of the hill. They were like black, quivering leaves in the moonlight.

"Let's go!" Paige cut into her thoughts. "It's already dark."

"My folks are gonna kill me," Jay Paul said, following Paige. "I told 'em I'd be back before dark."

"I'll catch up," Meggie called out, thankful for the moonlight.

Paige turned and gave her a questioning glance.

Meggie gave Paige the 'I-have-to-go-to-the-restroom' look and disappeared behind the big tree.

Meggie gazed up at the branches covered with nighthawks. The odd little "peent" wails and whooshing of the birds filled the night air. Suddenly she tripped over something near the base and went sprawling. Groping for her flashlight, her hand slid across the thing that had caught her foot—a wooden slab nearly buried in vines and bird droppings. *Huh? What the...?* Grabbing her flashlight, she pulled the weeds and grass aside, trying to get a better look.

Her flashlight shone on a crudely carved word on the wooden slab. Trembling with excitement, she knelt down, trying to see, but she couldn't quite make it out. The rot of time and wind had taken its toll. Her thoughts raced. *Was this a grave marker?* she wondered. *Is this a grave?* Then suddenly it hit her mind. WOOD YOU FOLLOW ME TO THE NIGHTHAWKS. UNDER AND DOWN. BUT WAIT FOR THE MOON. *Whoa! Wait a minute—is this the last part of the clue?* Her mind reeled beneath the whirring hum of the little bull bats over her head. *Not under the Nighthawk Mine, but the* NIGHTHAWKS! UNDER THE NIGHTHAWKS. *Under this tree, under the* WOOD *marker...*

UNDER AND DOWN.

But wait for the moon...

Livery Stable

CHAPTER 12

Dizzy Discovery

"Paige! Paige!" Meggie yelled, racing back down toward her friend and
Jay Paul. "You'll never believe it. *Never!*"

Paige and Jay Paul stood under the bright moon. "What's wrong?"
Paige asked, "Did you fall in an outhouse or something? You're filthy."
She plugged her small upturned nose and frowned.

"No!" Meggie said breathlessly, trying to brush the gunk off her
cutoffs and tank top. Her ponytail swayed, her eyes flashed. "The clue!
I think I've uncovered the last part of the clue!"

Paige's chin dropped.

"Where?" Jay Paul asked, his eyes boring into Meggie now.

Meggie glanced at Paige. *Should we tell him?* she wondered.

"You said you don't care if you ever find the gold," he said to Paige,
then to Meggie. "Well, I do. I've been looking for it ever since we came
to Nighthawk three summers ago."

"I changed my mind," Paige said.

Meggie stifled a giggle.

His shoulders fell.

"But you did save our lives." It was Paige again.

Meggie caught her breath. Yes, Paige was right, she realized. If it weren't for Jay Paul, they wouldn't even be here. "Guess we'd be still be lying at the bottom of the Nighthawk Mine if it hadn't been for you."

"What'd you find?" Jay Paul moved closer.

Meggie threw up her hands, gesturing for him to back off. "Okay. A grave, only I'm not sure it's a grave."

His brown hair caught the moon's reflection as he tipped his head skeptically. "So—go on. What's a grave got to do with the last part of the clue? There are graves all over this valley and these hills."

"I almost tripped over this old wood thing, like a grave marker— under the nighthawk tree. WOOD...UNDER...get it?"

"How do you know it's a grave marker?" Paige gripped her arm.

"I don't know for sure, except there was a name or something carved on it. I couldn't make it out. The thing's half rotten and besides that, it's buried in a bunch of bird gunk and weeds." She grimaced, and brushed her arms and cutoffs once more.

"Couldn't you read just one word at least?" It was Jay Paul now.

"No."

Paige glanced over her shoulder. She heard a noise coming from behind a ledge to her right. She motioned Meggie and Jay Paul quiet.

"Let's go." Jay Paul said quietly, grabbing Meggie's arm. He squeezed it tight. He had heard it too.

"But, the gold!" Meggie whispered hoarsely.

"Shhhh!" Jay Paul said. "We split. Now."

"Maybe we can come back tomorrow, huh?"

"Fat chance," Paige muttered. "We're probably gonna be in big trouble when we get back. The big-league type of trouble, Meggie."

And Paige was right. Except it was worse than they thought. As they neared the foot of the mountain, Meggie saw the flashing red and blue lights of the sheriff vehicles and rescue units. Some of the lights were flashing over near the Caaba Mine to their right. Aunt Abby was pretty relaxed most of the time, but from the looks of things, this time might be an exception. Meggie swallowed a lump stuck like a plank in her throat.

"They probably think we fell in one of the mines," Jay Paul spoke first, waving his flashlight to signal that everything was okay.

Meggie waved her flashlight, calling out over the faint barking of the K-9 rescue dogs. "We're here!" she yelled. "We're up here!"

In minutes, they found themselves surrounded by the worried Okanogan County sheriff and rescue units, Aunt Abby, and Jay Paul's parents.

"We fell into this hole up in that Nighthawk mine," Paige explained, looking fairly innocent.

Aunt Abby was the only one who didn't have a troubled look on her face. "Another one, Paige?"

Paige shrugged. "Meggie fell in, too. But Jay Paul saved us. He hooked our rope with this big tree branch and tied it around a rock so we could climb out. Thank heavens there weren't any snakes, Aunt Abby."

Meggie felt relieved that it was Paige and not her doing the explaining. For some reason, Paige seemed to know how to get out of trouble better than most kids. She noticed that Mr. and Mrs. Leeberg motioned Jay Paul aside.

"But it was worth it," Paige went on. "You'll never believe what Meggie found. "

Meggie shot a sharp 'keep-your-mouth-shut' glance in Paige's direction.

Paige got the message.

"Yes?" The sheriff questioned. "Did you find something unusual?"

"Uh, yeah," Meggie replied. "I found this awesome tree just covered with nighthawks. You know, those little birds they named this town after? Anyway, I stood under it and…"

"It looks like you rolled around under it," Aunt Abby interrupted, whisking Paige and Meggie toward the van. "Thank you for your help," she said, turning to the sheriff and rescue personnel who were all relieved the kids were safe.

Even the dogs seemed happy. Meggie noticed that they were wagging their tails and running around like they were on vacation.

"I'm sorry for all the trouble," Aunt Abby added, climbing into her vehicle.

"See you tomorrow," Meggie called to Jay Paul, hoping they wouldn't all be grounded for the rest of the summer.

When they got back to the campsite, Meggie knew they were going to have to explain what happened. She knew they had to start at the beginning and not skip details, including the ghost. Aunt Abby had that 'I-want-every-detail' look in her eyes. By the time she and Paige finished their story, Meggie hoped their ghost town detective days weren't over forever.

"I should take you home tonight," Aunt Abby told them, getting up and walking around the camp stove. "Or lock you up in the Nighthawk Hotel and force you to eat vegetables and field mice for a week!"

Meggie glanced at Paige whose face had already turned mouse green.

"I won't, though, because I'm curious myself," Aunt Abby went on, pushing her frizz of hair off her forehead. "I'd like to go up there with you and take a look."

Meggie's heart leaped with joy. "Oh, Aunt Abby! You are the best. The best!"

Paige couldn't speak.

"And soft headed," Aunt Abby added with a faint smile crinkling her lips. "Now get to bed so we can be on our way early tomorrow morning. We have to leave Nighthawk by late afternoon if we're going to spend the night with your Aunt Sharon in Wenatchee."

"I wonder if Jay Paul got into trouble," Meggie said to Paige as soon as they were in their sleeping bags with the light out. "It seems only fair he gets to go, too."

"Maybe his folks aren't like Aunt Abby," Paige said to her.

"Maybe not."

"If that was my mom, I'd definitely be grounded for the summer," Paige went on. "But my dad..."

"Yeah?" Paige was talking about her dad again. It was the second time in the last two days.

"I—I think my dad might've been more like Aunt Abby. But I'm not positive."

"Can you see him if you want?" Meggie asked, wondering why Paige never saw her dad after her parents' divorce.

Paige nodded in the shadows. "Mom says it's up to me, but I haven't really wanted to. Not after he left us like that."

Meggie didn't have parents who got divorced, so she didn't understand exactly how Paige felt. But maybe she'd feel the same way if that had happened with her dad. "Do you think about him sometimes?"

"Sometimes. But I stopped reading his letters a long time ago, and now Mom just sends the birthday and Christmas presents back, too. I kept that one necklace I told you about, though. Remember?"

Yes. Meggie remembered what happened in Bodie. Except for what happened in that ghost town, though, it didn't seem like Paige cared much about her dad at all. Meggie always figured Paige could take him or leave him. But then, she was sort of like that about a lot of things. Maybe that explained why Paige always seemed so brave and strong on the outside. But maybe on the inside, it was a different story.

"Do you think Mr. Cooksey might be something like my dad, Meggie?"

"Your dad's not that old."

"That's not what I mean."

Meggie shook her head. She didn't understand.

"I mean, maybe Mr. Cooksey's something like my dad and—and Cassie's like me."

Meggie suddenly realized what Paige meant "Like maybe your dad was kicking up his heels too much? Sorta like Mr. Cooksey?"

Paige nodded. "I'm not sure. Mom doesn't want to talk about it."

"Maybe it was different with your dad, Paige"

"Maybe." She shrugged. "Either way though, I still think I know something about how Cassie feels."

Meggie blinked in the shadows, listening to her best friend.

"I wonder where she is now, Meggie?"

"You mean, Cassie?"

"Uh huh. I wonder if she misses him now. Or if she just feels mad and never wants to see him again. Maybe that's why she never came back to Nighthawk."

Meggie could hear the sadness in Paige's voice. She didn't know what to say. Except Cassie would be a lot older than Paige. She might even be old enough to be a grandma by now. But it did seem weird. Why hadn't she ever come back to see her father? What had happened to Julian Cooksey's little girl?

"'Night, Meggie," Paige said, scrunching down in her sleeping bag.

Meggie knew Paige had finished talking. She'd said a lot tonight, though. More than ever. "'Night, Paige," Meggie replied. Maybe she didn't know Paige as well as she thought, but she was still her best friend in the world. Meggie closed her eyes, glad they were going to go on being best friends instead of dead bodies at the bottom of a mine shaft.

Meggie felt thankful for Aunt Abby, too, although she suspected that hanging out with her on a year-round basis might be a little bit dangerous. A few ghost towns every summer felt just right. Aunt Abby understood what was—and what wasn't, important. She could hardly wait until morning.

But it was hard to sleep and it wasn't just because of their discovery under the nighthawk tree. Meggie couldn't get Paige's words off her mind. And she couldn't stop thinking about old Mr. Cooksey, either. Nobody deserved to be brushed off the way she had done that morning. Meggie listened to the wind rustle the locust trees overhead, wishing she'd listened to one of his stories at least. She closed her eyes and forced her thoughts back to the Nighthawk Mine.

The moon

The moon

BUT WAIT FOR THE MOON...AND SOON...

CHAPTER 13

The Grave?

Jay Paul stood talking to Aunt Abby first thing the next morning.

"You didn't get grounded?" Meggie asked him as she crawled out of the tent.

"No. That's because I saved your lives. My mom thinks I'm a hero."

Paige stood there, rolling her eyes heavenward.

"They said I can't go back up to the Nighthawk Mine without an adult, though," he told them.

"You're in luck," she grinned, smoothing her rumpled cutoffs and shirt. "Aunt Abby is going up with us." Meggie wondered if she should explain that her aunt probably wasn't the kind of adult his folks were thinking about. Oh well. If she tried to explain, it probably wouldn't come out right.

Aunt Abby handed the girls a box of cereal and some paper bowls, then turned to Jay Paul. "Tell your parents I'll take you up with us," she said, "but I'd like for us to be on our way before it gets too hot."

"Yesss!" he said, dashing off. "Be right back!"

By the time Jay Paul returned, they had finished eating and were ready to go.

"If it's a grave, we have to cover it back up and leave it alone," Aunt Abby explained, slipping a small shovel and trawl into her backpack. "Gravediggers can be prosecuted by the Law."

"What if it isn't a grave?" Paige asked, heading across the field toward the bridge.

Meggie knew Paige meant the gold. She glanced back over her shoulder at the livery stable, wondering if they were being watched again. Jay Paul told them it wasn't him in the livery stable. So who was it? If it was gold buried up there at the Nighthawk Mine and somebody figured they were hot on the trail, they needed to be careful. *Very, very careful.* She motioned for Paige to keep her voice lower.

Aunt Abby smiled. "If it isn't a grave, then we'll decide what to do when we get there. It may be an important discovery," she said, adjusting her straw hat, "and then again, it may not."

Meggie drew a sharp breath, listening to her aunt talk about some of the possible artifacts they might find. Arrowheads. Miners equipment. Old bottles and dishes left over from the settlement. *Or Haggerty's gold,* she wanted to add. But she didn't. She just kept listening to her aunt, thankful they were getting a chance to come back up here and find out. Either way, she was glad to have her aunt along, just in case somebody might be following them. Nobody messed with Aunt Abby and came out right-side up.

They moved at a fast pace across the bridge and up the mountain, and before the noon sun crested, they had reached the Nighthawk Mine.

"Well, look at this!" Aunt Abby exclaimed, her eyes scanning the mineshaft and outbuildings scattered around. "Tucked away as neat as can be."

Meggie hurried over to the nighthawk tree and sighed with relief. The slab of wood was exactly where she'd left it. *Exactly.* "It's over here!" she called, motioning them over. Meggie felt thankful someone or something hadn't dug it up and taken it while they slept. Nobody except the nighthawks had been here. Yanking some vines and weeds aside, she carefully pulled it out of its moldy, dung-covered resting place.

They leaned closer, trying to read the crudely carved letters scrawled across the wooden slab. "S C R..." Paige said slowly, carefully.

"Doesn't look like a grave marker, but maybe it is," Aunt Abby told them.

"No," Paige put in quickly. "No, it's not a grave. I can tell."

Meggie turned to Paige who was talking like she was an authority on graves.

"Well, you can start digging, but be careful," Aunt Abby said, pulling the fold-up shovel out of her backpack. "If it is a grave, we'll have to leave it alone." She handed the shovel to Meggie. "When or *if* you hit something, ease up. You don't want to damage it with that shovel."

"Maybe it's that old miner, Haggerty, who got run outta town," Jay Paul put in. "The story says he wanted to be buried near Nighthawk but nobody's ever found his grave."

"No, those letters don't spell 'Haggerty,'" Meggie told him, ramming the shovel into the earth. "Paige is probably right when she said it's not a grave."

"If you get tired, I'll take over," he went on. "If it is a grave, we're probably going to have to dig pretty deep."

If he had any brains, he'd stop the grave talk, Meggie said through gritted teeth, wishing she could stuff his mouth with some of the dirt she was unearthing. Aunt Abby was one hundred percent archaeologist and could be real strict about breaking rules and digging where they weren't supposed to be digging.

"So...how do you *know* it's not a grave?" Jay Paul challenged, arching one brow.

Meggie bristled, giving him the 'if-it-was-a-grave-then-we'd-have-to-stop-digging' look.

Jay Paul got the message. He picked up the slab of wood and moved it out of the shadows into the sunlight where he could see more clearly. Paige followed him.

"S-C-R..." he muttered, scraping away some of the dirt and gunk with his knife. But he couldn't make out the rest of the words and neither could Paige.

Meggie dug on and on like she planned to reach China by late afternoon.

"Here, let me..." Jay Paul said finally, taking the shovel from Meggie.

Willingly, Meggie handed it over, wiping some dirt and sweat from her face. The smell was *terrible*. The nighthawks were definitely doing more than just roosting in this tree for over a hundred years, she realized. *They are also using it for an outhouse. Ugh.*

She walked over to Paige who was still trying to make out the word on the wooden marker. Aunt Abby was off poking around the miners' shacks with her trowel. Meggie knew her aunt could save a whole lot of time if she'd just use a shovel, but understood that archaeologists mostly use trowels so they won't damage any valuable artifacts.

"Okay, let me see if I can figure it out," Meggie said, taking the slab from Paige. She held it out to the sun, adjusting her glasses. "Okay...S-C-R... Whoa—wait a minute. Look, Paige. That's the letter 'F' isn't it?

83

Yes! The last letter is an 'F,' don't you think?" Her hands began to tremble. "And maybe two 'F's'...? Sure, look! That's it."

Paige nodded. "I thought so too, but I wasn't positive."

"Okay, then..." Meggie went on, her knuckles whitening as she gripped the thing tighter. "S-C-R..FF Scriff? Scraff? Scruff?"

"SCRUFF! Whoa, yes, that's it!" Paige exploded, pointing to the faint trace of a U in the center. "Yes, I'll bet anything that's it!" Her finger scraped away more gunk.

Meggie agreed. "But what's a Scruff?"

Jay Paul dropped the shovel and ran to where Meggie and Paige stood. "You guys figure it out?" He almost fell over his big feet.

Meggie nodded so fast she thought her ponytail was going to fly off her head.

"Yeah!" Paige told him. "Scruff!"

"Scruff?" Jay Paul frowned. "What's that mean? What's a Scruff?"

"I'm not sure," Meggie replied, wishing the word had sounded a little bit more important.

Paige raced back to the site and started digging again. Suddenly the shovel hit something. "Get over here!" she called out.

Hugging the wooden object close, Meggie raced over to Paige. Jay Paul followed in her dust. Meggie glanced over her shoulder, realizing that her aunt hadn't heard the thump of the shovel when it hit the object. But that was okay. They couldn't stop now.

What is it?" Jay Paul asked, nearly knocking Paige over.

"The SCRUFF, what else?" Paige replied, pushing some dirt aside.

"Here, let me—" Jay Paul said, trying to take the shovel from Paige. But before he could make his move, Paige had uncovered the small rectangular container.

Meggie caught her breath and stared at the small object. *A suitcase?* she wondered, inching closer. *Or was it a miniature trunk?* The container was about the size of three shoeboxes, except it had a handle.

"Cool!" Paige exclaimed, kneeling down and trying to get a closer look.

"At least it's not a grave," Meggie said, trying to brush the dirt aside.

Paige agreed. "Yeah, too small to be a coffin."

"Is it heavy?" Jay Paul's words trembled with excitement. Hope.

Meggie knew he meant the gold. "No," she said, trying not to show her own disappointment as she pulled the half-rotted thing out of the earth. "No, it's not heavy at all."

"What a bummer," he snorted.

But Meggie scarcely heard him. Fingering the rough, tweedy surface of the rotting leather, she noticed two rusty metal latches.

"It looks like a suitcase," Jay Paul put in. "Well, at least let me help open it."

"Whoa. Wait just one minute." Paige turned to Jay Paul.

"You found the clue, you found the marker and you figured out SCRUFF," he said to them both. "The least you can do is let me in on the last part."

"But, this is the most exciting part of all," Paige held her ground.

"Yeah, but if it wasn't for me, you'd both be down in that mine turning into bat food."

Meggie cringed, then looked at Paige. Paige looked at Meggie.

"Okay," Paige said, moving aside. "But we open this thing together, Jay Paul Leeberg. Together!"

Meggie nodded in agreement, her heart thumping with excitement.

Jay Paul crouched down, gripping the strange little object. Together they set it on the ground. By this time Aunt Abby had heard the commotion and walked over to where they were gathered. "Doesn't look like a burial casket to me," she said.

"Or the gold," Jay Paul added cheerlessly.

Meggie struggled to pry open the copper latches with an old tool she'd found near the mine entrance. Paige and Jay Paul held it firmly.

"Looks like a suitcase," Paige said. "There's one something like this in my grandma's attic, except this one is a lot smaller than Grandma's."

"It's called a grip," Aunt Abby said, walking up from behind.

"A what?" Meggie paused and looked up.

"My grandmother had one almost exactly like this," her aunt explained. "Just a small suitcase. An overnight bag, except she always called it a grip."

"Oh good. Then it *is* old, right?" Paige asked.

"Yes. I'm surprised at how well preserved it is, though," her aunt said, kneeling closer. "It's probably due to the copper latches and handle. You remember how copper preserves nearly anything it touches."

Yes, Meggie remembered the diary they had found in the ghost town of Bodie. She remembered the old copper tin that had kept it hidden for so many years. And here they were again. This time with another treasure. Or was it? Was it just an empty old suitcase some miner had tossed away. Meggie's pulse quickened as she forced the latches open with the tool. Slowly, carefully they opened the grip.

Meggie drew a deep breath.

A scruffy little teddy bear with brown glass eyes stared up at them. Beside the bear lay a squat, round copper container with a small, black lid on top.

"Scruff..." Paige said, reaching down and stroking the fur.

A dumb little teddy bear, Meggie said silently, hoping her disappointment didn't show. *So much for the treasure.*

"Well, I'll be—a child's toy," Aunt Abby said, standing over them. "Your clue must have been the antics of a child." She took off her straw hat and knelt down. "But look what else we have here. Not a toy."

Jay Paul picked up the container. "FILL TO BRIM." He read the embossed words on the lid as he tried to unscrew it.

"A bed warmer," Aunt Abby told them. "Yesterday's version of the hot water bottle."

"Hot water bottle? What's that?" Jay Paul asked.

"Try a heating pad?" Aunt Abby replied.

Paige made a face. "Weird. Heating pad is fine, but you wouldn't catch me with one of those funky little tin turtles in my bed! No way."

Meggie giggled.

"It's not tin, it's copper," Aunt Abby told them. The copper is the reason everything has been so well preserved."

Meggie took the teapot-sized object from Jay Paul and tried to unscrew the lid. *This is weird. A teapot with a spout on the top instead of the side.* Suddenly the seal snapped. "Oops. Got it!"

"Anything in there?" It was Jay Paul. He almost cracked heads with Paige.

Meggie reached in but the opening was too small for her hand. She tipped it upside down and a small, carefully folded piece of paper fell out. Her throat caught.

"What is it?" Jay Paul exploded. "The clue that leads to the gold?"

Paige almost knocked him over, trying to get a closer look at the piece of paper in Meggie's hand. "Be careful, Meggie."

Meggie tried to keep her hands steady as she read the scrawl across the folded note.

PAPA.

CHAPTER 14

Buried Treasure

"Papa—?" Paige said the word slowly, turning to Meggie. "Oh Meggie, you don't think…"

Meggie didn't know what to think. Trembling fingers unfolded the fragile piece of paper, staring at the same, familiar scrawl—the same handwriting used on the note she had found in the curtain rod back at the Nighthawk Hotel. Jay Paul breathed down one side of her neck, Paige down the other.

"*Dear Papa,*" Meggie began, " *Mama says we haf to leave you. She says it be best. I writ you and hid it in my room for you to find. Scruff will keep my letter safe till you find it in our speshul place under the Night-hawk tree. I want you to kno that I love you and thet I always will no matter what you did. I heared Mama tell Uncle George thet we are going to Mrs. Sippi. I hope she is nice. I will miss you even more than Scruff. Love furever, Cassie*

"Cassie!" Paige exploded, nearly knocking Jay Paul and Meggie over. "That's Mr. Cooksey's little girl!"

Meggie could hardly believe it. Her mind reeled, her pulse

pounded. *Oh my gosh! It was Cassie. Cassie wrote that clue and hid it in the curtain rod up in that hotel. Cassie climbed this mountain and buried her letter—her secret.* Tears stung Meggie's eyes as she stared at the note in her hand.

"Aunt Abby!" Paige said, jumping up. "Mr. Cooksey's little girl wrote this! She loves him! No matter what he did, she..." Paige's words flooded with tears and she couldn't go on.

"She's not a little girl now," Aunt Abby said, placing her hand on Paige's shoulder. "Cassie could be a grandmother by this time."

Meggie gazed into her aunt's face, then turned to Paige who struggled to hold back her feelings. Meggie wanted to hug Paige but she couldn't with Jay Paul standing there. Paige almost never had wet eyes and a lower lip that quivered. Meggie watched her best friend walk away and wished there was something she could say. Or do.

But there was a lot going on inside Meggie too. Yet it was different. Would she ever be able to make up for the awful way she had acted toward that old man? Could he ever forgive her for being such a jerk? *Oh Mr. Cooksey, I'm sorry*, Meggie said silently, wishing she hadn't been so rude. Meggie knew she would never, ever treat an old person—*any* person like that again.

Just wait, Mr. Cooksey. Just wait 'till you find out what we've got for you! Meggie could hardly hold back the feelings inside—the happiness and sadness rushing together in the hot circle of wind there on the mountain above Nighthawk. The letter in her hand was so much better than gold. *So much better.*

"You Ghostowners have made quite a discovery!" Aunt Abby said, shaking her head and smiling. She plopped her hat on her frizz of hair and hitched her nylon backpack over her shoulder, motioning them down. "I think Julian Cooksey is in for quite a surprise!"

Meggie grinned and nodded, wiping the happy tears from her eyes.

But Paige didn't say anything. She just walked behind them, holding the small moldy suitcase in one hand.

Jay Paul brought up the rear. "I wonder if there's still gold in that mine," he said, glancing back.

"I doubt it, but if there was, Mr. Cooksey would probably know about it," Aunt Abby told him, stepping sure-footedly down the incline.

"I don't think so," Jay Paul told her. "At least not anymore. I mean a lot of old people forget things. Like sometimes my grandfather puts milk in the cupboard and feeds his cat birdseed. Stuff like that."

Aunt Abby paused and turned, giving him a blank look. Meggie figured it might be because Aunt Abby did things like that, too. Jay Paul would have to think of something else.

They hiked on.

"I do feel kinda sorry for him, though," Jay Paul went on. "I don't think he's got a family or much of anything anymore."

Well he might now, Meggie said silently, hoping against hope they could find Cassie.

"His roof leaks and every time Dad climbs up to fix it, the whole roof practically caves in and almost kills my dad."

Meggie stepped over the flume zig-zagging back and forth down the mountain, remembering his house when she had gone looking for rope to rescue Paige. It looked like it was about ready to fall down in the next wind. Meggie had almost broken her leg when she stepped on to the porch and fell through.

"Dad says somebody's going to have to take him home or put him in a nursing home, or do something pretty soon before he starves or freezes to death," Jay Paul continued, his brown hair waving in the warm wind. "We never stay up here during the winter and he won't go home with us. It gets real cold up here at Nighthawk. He gets stuck up here in the snow for months on end sometimes."

"Well maybe that's going to change," Paige said, wiping her eyes quickly with the back of her hand. "The part about the family, I mean." Her chin wasn't quivering now.

Meggie nodded, feeling that same hope. She'd been thinking about Cassie and wondered if they could find her. Uncle George and Mrs. Sippi weren't much to go on. Then suddenly it hit her mind. *Wait a minute. Is Mrs. Sippi a state, instead of a person? Sure...Mississippi!* Meggie's thoughts reeled. *And if Cassie was only seven-years-old when she wrote that note, then maybe that's exactly what she'd think. Yes! Why not? Even though Mississippi was a long way off, maybe that was where Cassie and her mother had gone. And Uncle George, well—he might be anywhere. It was something to go on.* "Yesss!"

Meggie's hopes continued to surge ahead as she moved at a fast pace down the mountain. *Well, why not? If they found Cassie's message in the curtain rod and the letter under the Nighthawk Tree, then why couldn't they find her too?* Meggie held the fragile letter close, hoping and praying Cassie was still alive somewhere—hoping she hadn't given up hope when her father never came for her. *But why hadn't she tried to find him when she grew up?* Meggie wondered. *Had she been too young to remember Nighthawk? Did the memories just fade away, or did Cassie's mother want her to forget—even make it impossible for her to ever find her father?* They had to find out.

"Since he owns a lot of the land around Nighthawk, then maybe he could sell it and get a real neat house with a cook and maid and stuff," Paige said. "Then he wouldn't have to leave and go to a nursing home."

Meggie turned to Paige.

"Well he does own a lot of the land around here, Meggie. Why couldn't he just sell some of it, and get what he needs?"

"Nobody wants the land around here," Jay Paul told them. "My folks got our cabin and property real cheap from a lady in Loomis. I guess not many people want to hang out in a ghost town."

Except ghosts, Meggie said under her breath. With all the excitement of finding Cassie's treasure, she almost forgot about the ghost.

"Well, maybe he just likes it here," Paige said. "Maybe he's still waiting for Cassie."

"Well, he can't wait much longer. I mean, he's not going to make it another year," Jay Paul said. He took the lead now. "I don't know which is going to collapse first—him or his house."

Meggie agreed with Paige about Cassie. "I'll bet he's still hoping…" she said, but she couldn't finish. The words caught like barbed wire in her throat.

"I hope so, Meg," Aunt Abby put in, "but there's a strong chance we might not find Cassie. We'll do the best we can, but we can't get the old man's hopes up too high."

Meggie drew back and caught Paige's wide-eyed glance. She didn't want to hear her aunt's words. She still wanted to believe that even after all these years, they were still going to find his Cassie.

And was Jay Paul right? Was it better for Mr. Cooksey to be in a clean, safe place until then? Could he survive one more winter up here in Nighthawk?

And then she thought of the ghost. *The ghost.* She almost fell over a rock.

"What's wrong, Meggie?" Paige said quietly. "You just turned ten shades of gray."

"Uh..the ghost," she leaned close and whispered. "Did you forget about the ghost, Paige?"

"Huh? Hey, who cares? We're leaving Nighthawk, remember?"

"But Mr. Cooksey isn't."

"Oh yeah, I see what you're saying."

"Maybe it's better—safer—if Mr. Cooksey does get out of Nighthawk, Paige. I mean, with a ghost hanging around and all." Meggie and Paige hung back.

"But we're not sure about the ghost. I'll bet anything it was Jay Paul all the time."

"It wasn't Jay Paul in the hotel. I'm telling you, Paige, there is a ghost hanging around Nighthawk."

"We can't be *sure.*"

"Who else would've stolen my Mickey Mouse glasses? I mean, they just vanished into thin air. Weird stuff has been happening. I know it's a ghost now. It's been following us. Everywhere we go—everything we do. It's so crazy, Paige. First the hotel, then the livery stable, and last night—on the mountain. We need to get out of this place before something really bad happens, and maybe old Mr. Cooksey does too."

Paige's wide eyes held Meggie's gaze.

"And the gold," Meggie went on, "I don't even *care* about the gold anymore, do you?"

"Yeah. I mean no," Paige muttered, walking on down the mountain.

"Who cares if we have Arabian horses or phones in our rooms?"

Meggie told her.

"Mr. Cooksey probably doesn't even have a phone."

"I know," Meggie agreed, "and he probably doesn't have a CD player, either."

"He probably doesn't even know what a CD player *is*."

Meggie nodded in agreement.

"And, she loved him, Meggie," Paige said, her chin starting to quiver again. "Cassie loved her dad no matter what he did."

Meggie turned to Paige. Her friend was fighting back her feelings again, wasn't she? Maybe what happened to Cassie *was* a lot like what happened to Paige.

"Yeah," Meggie said finally. "I think Cassie loved him a lot." But that was all Meggie could think of to say. They walked the rest of the way down the mountain in silence, following Aunt Abby and Jay Paul across the bridge into Nighthawk at last.

Pausing, she glanced at Julian Cooksey's house in the distance and gripped Cassie's note tighter in her sweaty hand.

This is it, Paige. This is it....

Julian Cooksey's House

CHAPTER 15

The Ghost
of Nighthawk?

"Now remember," Aunt Abby said, "take it slow. We don't want to get his hopes too high, just in case."

"Does it matter?" Paige broke into her words. "Cassie loved him and—and maybe that's enough." Her short dark hair flew in her face and she tossed it away in that familiar, quick gesture.

Aunt Abby paused and looked down into Paige's dark, searching eyes. "Maybe you're right."

Paige set her chin and led the way toward the old house In a few minutes they were knocking on Julian Cooksey's door.

"Eh, what have we here?" the old man opened the door, struggling to keep it from falling off its hinges.

Jay Paul reached out to help as Mr. Cooksey smiled and invited everyone inside. "Reckon I haven't had company for a spell so you'll have to 'scuse the mess."

Meggie could hardly find a place to step in the cluttered old house. Dust and clothing and junk was lay everywhere. It looked as though it hadn't been cleaned since Cassie and her mother left some fifty years before. Meggie clutched the letter in her hand and glanced at Paige who gripped the little suitcase as though it was filled with gold.

"Eh, what have you there?" He glanced down at the small, dirt-covered object in Paige's hand.

"Oh, Mr. Cooksey!" Meggie cried, "It's..."

"What the—? That's Cassie's grip! That's my little Cassie's!"

Grinning, Paige held it out to the old man. "She buried it up at the mine," she said loudly. "The Nighthawk Mine!"

Julian Cooksey's stubbled chin dropped as he took it from her hands, opening it carefully and gazing inside. "Scruffy?" he said, his cracked lips trembling. "Cassie's little Scruff." The moist gray eyes crinkled as the old man stood there stroking the tattered little bear. "An' my foot warmer? What the—?"

"And here's a letter she wrote you," Meggie said, drawing a deep breath and handing him the carefully folded scrap of paper. She tried to speak loudly enough so that he could hear. "Plus, here's the note I found in the curtain rod up in the hotel." Meggie pulled the scrap of paper from her pocket. "It's the clue that led us to the Nighthawk tree where we dug up Scruff."

"Eh?" He seemed overwhelmed, staring at the letter, then the note in Meggie's hand. His gray, bristled chin quivered.

Meggie handed him the note from Cassie—the clue she had found in the curtain rod. "She hid it so well, we almost didn't find it."

He set the grip aside and unfolded the letter, straining to see—trying to read the child's scrawl. Meggie knew he was having trouble.

"Want me to read it to you, Mr. Cooksey?" Paige asked, reaching out her hand.

The old man nodded, handing her the letter and the scrap of paper, then hurried over to a table. He fumbled around for his hearing aids, placing one in each ear, then shuffled back to where they were standing, trying in vain to stop the noise. The whistling sounded like two little nighthawks stuck in his ears. "Dang plugs," he snorted, turning down the shrill little whistles. "Cain't order a decent thing from a catalog anymore."

Aunt Abby's chin fell. "A *catalog*?"

He nodded. "Twenty-five buckaroos I paid for these two worthless, oversized beans that do nothin' but whistle. Twenty five. You believe that? Nothin' but highway robbery."

Aunt Abby didn't answer. She just kept shaking her head in amazement.

"But enough of this nonsense," he went on. "The letter..."

Paige cleared her throat and began to read.

"Dear Papa, Mama says we haf to leave you. She says it be best." Paige paused, the letter trembling in her hand, but she went on. "I writ you and hid it in my room. Scruff will keep my letter safe till you find it in our speshul place under the Nighthawk tree. I want you to kno that I love you and thet I always will no matter what you did. I heared Mama tell Uncle George thet we are going to Mrs. Sippi. I hope she is nice. I will miss you Papa.

 Love furever, Cassie "

Meggie swallowed the tears that were backing up in her throat, then looked up into Julian Cooksey's face. She felt Paige's grip tighten on her arm and knew her friend felt the same way.

The old man stood there with tears rolling down his wrinkled cheeks. But he was smiling. "Little Cassie—little Cassie... " was all he could say, over and over. "My little Cassie girl."

Paige reached him first. Then Meggie. Even Aunt Abby found herself hugging the old man who was practically dancing by now. They were all hugging and jumping around so much, Jay Paul had to stop them for fear the floor would collapse. Meggie didn't know when she'd ever felt this happy. It beat ten Arabian horses. Ten!

Since his catalog hearing aids weren't working very well, explaining everything took a lot of time. Even though Meggie had a sore throat when they were through, it was worth it. Except it scared her to death the way he ended up dancing all over the shack. She was afraid they might have to call 911 and he didn't even have a phone.

"So you were after the Haggerty gold, eh?" Julian Cooksey chortled, grinning from ear to ear. His stringy gray hair framed his smile like a strange and wonderful crown.

"Yeah, pretty dumb, huh?" Paige laughed.

"Wal, I could tell you a story or two about Haggerty and Nighthawk," Julian Cooksey snorted, a twinkle in his gray-blue eyes. "Oh, yes I could."

"Oh, Mr. Cooksey—*would you*?" Meggie asked, pulling up a chair.

Paige grinned at Aunt Abby and Jay Paul, then pulled up another chair on the other side of the old man.

"But first things first," he said, fingering the letter his daughter had written fifty-three years before. "First, Cassie's letter."

"Yes," Aunt Abby smiled, pulling up a stool and getting a tablet and pen out of her nylon pack. Meggie could tell that her aunt was just as excited as they were.

"Mississippi. So that's where her mama took her."

"And who's Uncle George?" Meggie asked him.

"Eh?"

"Uncle George. Who's he?" she asked again.

"Millie's half brother," Julian Cooksey replied, shaking his head in amazement. "George Crook. Wouldn't give me the time of day, but cain't say as I blame him." The old man dropped his head and sighed. "People change, but sometimes mebbe it's too late."

"Maybe not, Mr. Cooksey," Paige said, reaching for his hand. "Maybe it's never too late."

The old man gazed wordlessly into Paige's wide brown eyes, then squeezed her hand.

Paige released her grip so that she could wipe some stray tears that were beginning to slip down her cheeks. And Julian Cooksey blew his nose with the dirtiest hankie Meggie had ever seen in her life.

"Anyhows," the old man snorted and went on, "George Crook and his wife lived outside a little town called Rolling Fork, I think it was. Yep, that's it. Rolling Fork, Mississippi. Dang blast, why didn't I think of that?" he muttered. "Almost forgot Millie had that half brother stuck down there."

"Then, you tried to find her?" Jay Paul asked.

"Did I try to find her?" He turned to Jay Paul like he was the most ignorant person on earth. "For years an years I tried, young man. Traveled everywheres lookin' for my little Cassie." He shook his old head back and forth, pursing his lips. "I'll be dad blamed. Never even thought of George Crook..."

"I wonder if she's been trying to find you all these years?" Paige said to him.

The old man looked down into her face and held her gaze. He didn't answer. Maybe he couldn't.

"Well, let's start with Rolling Fork," Aunt Abby said, jotting down the information on her tablet.

"Ah yes, Rolling Fork, Mississippi," he began. And Julian Cooksey didn't stop until he had told them every last detail about Cassie and her mother and the search that had never ended.

And when they all said goodbye, there wasn't a dry eye in the place. Meggie couldn't remember when she'd ever felt so good.

They walked over to the Leeberg's cabin with Jay Paul, telling his folks what had happened and agreeing to keep in touch and do everything they could to find Cassie Cooksey.

"In the meantime, we'll take care of Julian," the Leebergs assured them. They had been concerned about the old man for a long time, and were overwhelmed with the hopeful news.

"Next time you come back to Nighthawk," Jay Paul put in, "maybe you'll get to meet Cassie."

Meggie brushed the wind-blown hair from her face and nodded. Yes, they'd be back. She turned and walked away.

"Cassie might even help me find Haggerty's gold," he added with a grin. "But if I find it, I'll be sure and let you know. Who knows? I might even take you both into Chesaw for a treat. Y'know, a candy bar or two."

Meggie paused in her tracks and whirled around. "A *candy bar?*"

"Or two."

"Yesss, Jay Paul Leeburg. That's gonna make me *so* happy."

"Yeah," Paige agreed, "so happy, she might even give you a hug."

Meggie whirled around, almost knocking her over. "Paige."

"Uh—on second thought," Jay Paul said, "I think uh—I'll give the gold to Mr. Cooksey."

"Yeah, good idea," Paige grinned, jabbing Meggie in the ribs.

"See ya!" Jay Paul called out to Meggie and Paige.

"You do that again and next time I'll leave you in the well," she said to Paige as soon as they were out of earshot.

Paige grinned and shrugged, looking innocent as usual.

After Meggie had forgiven her, she began to think of all that had transpired in just two short days. So many good things had happened that she had almost forgotten about losing her Mickey Mouse glasses. But somehow it didn't matter as much, now. Because of her bonk on the head and the discovery of the clue in the curtain rod, Julian Cooksey might find his little girl again and have a better life.

"Won't it be cool if Jay Paul actually *does* find the gold, though?" Paige said. "I'll bet if he does, he'll probably give it to Mr. Cooksey, don't you think?"

Meggie nodded. "Then he could get hearing aids that don't whistle. And get his roof fixed and have all the food and stuff he needs." Meggie's throat caught.

"Delivered," Paige said. "Or he could buy his own truck and hire a guy to drive it."

Meggie felt so good inside.

"Do you know how much horse stuff you'd have to shovel *every day* if you had a horse, Meggie?"

"And kids who have CD's turned up too loud can go deaf. And if you were deaf, we couldn't talk on our phones under the covers every night, anyway."

It felt so good just thinking about the way everything kept falling into place.

"I'm gonna write him, Meggie," Paige said when they reached the van.

Meggie turned to Paige. "Mr. Cooksey? You're gonna write Mr. Cooksey?"

"No. My dad. I'm going to write to my dad." Paige drew a deep breath and threw her hair out of wide, glistening eyes.

"You are?"

"Yeah, I am."

Meggie didn't know what to say. Her throat tightened and tears stung her eyes.

"I'm really glad we came to Nighthawk," Paige went on, struggling to get the words to come out right. "I—I'm really glad I met Mr. Cooksey."

"Me too."

"He might be a lot like my dad, Meggie." Paige's eyes were brimming now. "But I just don't want it to turn out wrong for me and my dad like it almost did for them."

Meggie looked deep into her best friend's eyes. "It's not going to turn out wrong. For them. Maybe not for you, either. Cassie's coming back, I just know it, Paige. She's going to find her dad."

"So am I, Meggie."

Meggie grabbed Paige's hand and tried to speak but the words just weren't there.

"We need to be on our way," Aunt Abby called. She finished hitching up the trailer. "But, I have a feeling we'll be back," she laughed, walking up to the girls, motioning them into the van. "We've got another mystery to solve and I can't wait to come back after all the pieces start falling together!"

Meggie and Paige gazed into each others eyes and started grinning. They climbed into the van, starting down the rutted gravel road past the Nighthawk Hotel. Meggie shook her head, staring up at the window where they had seen the shadow just two days before.

"It was a ghost," she said to Paige.

"For *sure*?"

"Why else did my Mickey Mouse glasses disappear into thin air? The Leebergs weren't here that first night, so it wasn't Jay Paul. I'm telling you Paige, Nighthawk has a ghost. There's just too much that points to it."

"Maybe that was just Jay Paul in the livery stable, though. He *was* following us."

"Okay," Meggie replied, "but when we were coming down the mountain with Jay Paul last night, I'm positive I heard something behind us—following us."

"But that *could've* been a coyote or a rabbit, Meggie."

"Yeah, sure, maybe. But the hotel was definite. Someone or—some *thing* followed us—watched us. And it took my glasses."

Paige shrugged.

"Oh, there's Mr. Cooksey waving," Aunt Abby called back to the girls.

Meggie rolled down the window, watching the old man hurry down his rutted driveway, waving goodbye with his cane.

"Oh, isn't he the sweetest old man?" Paige said, leaning out the window and waving back. "And just look at him. He's almost running!"

"Goodbye, Mr. Cooksey!" she called out.

Meggie waved and tried to call out, but her goodbyes were stuck in her throat. The old man had a smile that stretched from ear to ear. Her eyes blurred up with happy tears. Then, she caught her breath and looked again.

Julian Cooksey was wearing her Mickey Mouse glasses.

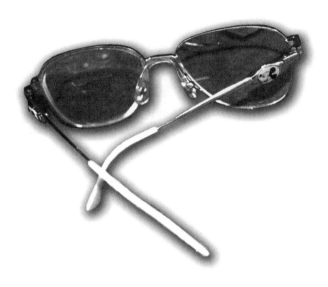

POSTSCRIPT

"Oh Papa. To think I just thought Nighthawk was a *bird*!" Cassie said, brushing her graying hair from smiling gray-blue eyes. "But I remembered the Nighthawk tree—our tree. I never, ever forgot. I remember how we'd sit under that tree with those little birds over our heads and you'd tell me all those wonderful stories. But who ever heard of a *town* called Nighthawk? And if only I'd got that first note to you. But I was positive you'd find it in my perfect hiding place in the curtain rod." She smiled.

Julian Cooksey grinned, blowing his nose with the clean hankie Cassie had just brought back from the laundromat at Chesaw. She smiled and placed her armful of laundry on the table.

"Got a few more of them stories," he chuckled.

"Good. But save some for your grandchildren. And your great grandchildren! You have eight now, you know. Eight little beanpoles kicking up the dust, just like their grandpa!" Cassie reached for a picture album she had brought all the way from Rolling Fork, Mississippi. "Here Papa, let me show you your family."

Julian Cooksey leaned closer, adjusting his glasses.

"By the way, Dad, I've been meaning to tell you something."

"Eh?" The old man gazed lovingly into his daughter's eyes.

"Your glasses. I think we'll have to do something about those glasses, don't you?"

He drew back and smiled from ear to ear. "Aren't they a marvel, Cassie girl?"

"Why yes, now that you mention it, I'd say they *are* something of a marvel."

"When I found these here glasses up in your old room at the hotel, everything started happenin', Cassie girl. One miracle after another—all leading straight to you." He took off the Mickey Mouse glasses and stroked each mouse gently with his old hand.

Cassie stared at the little mice and the pink wire frames that were three sizes too small, then looked up into her father's face. Her eyes blurred as she spoke, "Yes Papa, they are a marvel. We'll have to take good care of these glasses."

"Now by cracky," he snorted, "let's heat some water and fill up that copper bottle you buried. Scruff had it long enough." Julian Cooksey leaned over and kissed his daughter on the cheek. "Fifty-three years is a long time, Cassie girl. One more of these dang blast Nighthawk winters, and my feet would have froze plum off." He blew his nose and placed the glasses back on his old smile-crinkled face.

Mickey Mouse was smiling too.

AUTHOR'S NOTE

The idea of the note in the curtain rod came from an experience in my own childhood. Right after the Pearl Harbor attack of World War II, families on the West Coast prepared for an air attack with daily blackouts and air raid drills. Terrified, I wrote a letter to God and hid it in a curtain rod. Just in case our house was bombed, I wanted him to know that I loved him, that I'd been pretty good most of the time, and if he didn't mind, I'd like to go to heaven. Many years later during some remodeling, my mother found the tender, childish scrawl of a seven-year-old when the note dropped out of the curtain rod.